LAUGHTER THAT TURNED
THE WIND

VANESSA WARD

LAUGHTER THAT TURNED THE WIND

First published in 2021
Copyright © Vanessa Ward
Perth, Australia
ISBN 978-0-6453097-0-6
Edited by Ingrid Waltham
Designed by Luke Ward
Cover Photo by Luke Ward
Printed in Australia by IngramSpark

CONTENTS

CONTENTS

CONTENTS

CONTENTS

DEDICATION

I dedicate this book to all those who I love and who choose to walk beside me – my family and friends. In particular, to four extremely special humans who mean everything to me – my loving husband, John Ward, and our three beautiful children, Justin, Luke and Natalie. And of course my delightful grandson Jaxon, who inspires the child in me and reminds me to see the world and life through the eyes of a child – in its purest form.

Each of you has taught me that every human being is unique, that love inspires us, and that I would not be who I am today if not for each and every one of you.

Each of us is perfectly imperfect, and that is perfectly fine! The imperfect perfect is something we can all identify with. Parts of us are perfect, and some a little less so. We can choose to work on them or leave them just as they are. I choose you all just the way you choose to be and are happy to be.

Thank you for being accepting of who I am and allowing me to be a part of your story. I hope this story takes you on your own journey, to where we can all appreciate that it is our differences that allow us to live a unique life and have a positive impact on others.

This book is my gift to you. Hold it close and know my heart is in every word and my heart belongs to each of you.

Love you today, tomorrow and forever.

Vanessa Ward

In memory of my father,
Glen Evan Matson, 1936-2021

NEW NEIGHBOURS

Primrose stood in the lounge and watched as a moving truck pulled into the driveway next door, followed quickly by a beaten-up Volkswagen kombi pulling in behind. The back door slid open and two children with bare feet and long hair spilled out onto the driveway. Spilled out was right; they pushed and shoved and rolled onto the pavement, before pulling themselves up with shouts of laughter and racing towards the front door. Behind them, a slim woman with waist-length blonde hair jumped out of the passenger's side and raced just as enthusiastically to the front door. She inserted the key, twisted it and then disappeared inside. Rather more slowly, an unkempt long-haired male, sporting a bare chest along with his bare feet, whistled lazily as he strolled towards the door, glancing up and down the street before joining the others inside.

Primrose was spellbound by the eclectic bunch that had burst into this peaceful, tidy little neighbourhood. She called to her husband George to come quickly. He poked his head into the room and was bombarded by her chattering on about hippies moving in and changing the neighbourhood. George said little, merely nodding where appropriate.

The moving van let down its ramp and men started moving large boxes and pieces of furniture inside. Two children around the same age as Christian and Annabelle, Primrose's own children, darted in front and behind the men as they worked tirelessly and quickly to unload the contents of the truck. The children were loud, happy and, as Primrose stated loudly in a haughty voice, were 'running amuck'.

George decided he would go and mow the front lawn to make an appearance and maybe get a chance to introduce himself to the new neighbours. Primrose could not contain her curiosity and soon appeared beside him in the garage.

She spoke quietly to George. "I suppose the polite thing to do is invite them in for a barbecue if they are free."

George lifted his hand and waved tentatively as he saw his new neighbour heading towards his car.

"Hi," the neighbour called out in response. "How are you? I'm Handel, we're your new neighbours. Awesome day to move house, hey!"

Handel wandered over and, with a wide-open smile beaming with bright white even teeth, shook George's hand strongly. Primrose did not know where to look as he thrust his hand and hairy tanned chest towards her.

They were then joined by the woman, her long fair hair moving gently around her face in the breeze. Her sea-blue eyes were smiling as she introduced herself.

"Hi, I'm Sunshine – Sunnie - and these two are Rae and Cee."

Two happy, sun-kissed faces smiled at Primrose and spoke in unison as they each confidently shook Primrose's hand. "Nice to meet you."

Primrose was impressed. *These children have manners,* she thought, surprised at this in view of their brightly coloured and mismatched clothing.

George asked Handel if he and his family would like to join them in the early evening for a Friday barbecue. "No fuss, just steaks and salad."

"Love to!" was the response. "We'll bring a few drinks. See you around five? We should have most of the main furniture in place by then. Will be nice to put our feet up and have a yarn."

The glare of the summer sun had started to soften as Primrose began preparing the meat and gathering plates. Her thoughts were running wild. Her life so far had been filled with conservative, Christian individuals who lived their lives by the rules of the Bible. Conservative discussions, conservative dress, and living as a wife and husband 'should'. Their roles were clearly defined and their life was lived in a traditional, orderly fashion. Routine was paramount. The children were expected to do their chores, contribute to family life and serve within their church and extended community. There were rules, and on no account should rules be broken.

George and Primrose were well respected within the church and gave their time generously to those in need. They realised that life had been kind to them, and they had a duty to care for others less well-off. They also had strict rules of protocol when it came to how their children must behave: no swearing, no disrespecting one's elders, and at all times children should be 'seen and not heard'. They believed children have much to learn from their elders, and must not openly question them, even if they believed what they had been told was not correct. Both age and gender must override youth: the male is the head of the house; a role his son would inevitably repeat in his own family, with his own wife. It may sound old-fashioned to some, but it was how George and Primrose had been brought up in their own families, and they saw no reason to change the status quo.

To Primrose, these new neighbours screamed no rules, no boundaries, no respect and no morals. Why did she think this, after a mere five-minute meeting? Was it just their appearance? Sure, they had long hair – all of them! - their clothes were every colour of the rainbow, and their feet were bare. Yet despite this, they appeared open, warm and polite.

Primrose's head ached as she realised these people were already challenging her rigid views. *What have we done?* she thought. She could see absolutely no good coming out of welcoming them into her world. They would have nothing in common, and nothing to gain from befriending such a mismatched group of hippies. How would she survive living next door to these people? They were unlike anyone she had ever met before.

THE BARBECUE

The doorbell rang. Primrose quickly primped her hair as she dashed past the mirror to let them in. She hoped Annabelle and Christian had heard the bell, as they knew the house rules. It was polite to come out of your room and greet your guests as they arrived. Thankfully, on cue, both bedroom doors opened and the siblings joined the others on the patio. Annabelle collected iced tea from the fridge and glasses and set them on the tablecloth.

Laughter entered the home the minute the guests arrived, like a warm breath of fresh sea air sweeping through the house and settling into the backyard.

Annabelle had felt flustered the moment she was introduced to Rae. He looked like he had just stepped out of the sea and onto the golden sand, his long blond hair falling to his shoulders in waves. *This was not the typical type of family we normally entertain on a Friday evening,* Annabelle thought. She suddenly felt a little dreary in her knee-length floral dress and hair neatly brushed into a ponytail. As their eyes met, she couldn't help but notice his wide smile, brilliant blue eyes and tanned face. Her heart started racing, warming her face and colouring her cheeks.

She was so transfixed she almost forgot her manners. That would not go down well with her mother. She saw Primrose looking at her and recognised the look instantly. *Behave.* Annabelle offered the guests iced tea.

"Oh, thanks Annabelle." Rae responded with ease. Feeling relaxed, he pulled a packet of herbal cigarettes from his pocket. He immediately tucked them away again - but not before Primrose and Annabelle noticed. Rae felt awkward - he not only knew smoking was unhealthy, but it seemed inappropriate in this setting, in the home of his new neighbours, and he didn't want to offend. And to be honest, even though they were herbal, he knew they were disapproved of even by his liberal-thinking parents.

Primrose's face began to redden. Annabelle could tell her mother was trying to hide her shock and horror. Primrose detested cigarettes. She also noticed Handel and Sunnie had brought beer and wine, both of which were now being blatantly and casually displayed in front of the precious daughter she had groomed her whole life to be obedient and abstinent. She had never had to tolerate this before; it was not the normal behaviour among their small circle of friends.

Without warning, Primrose was being exposed to a whole new world in her own home. It seemed overwhelming, and she had no idea what her response should be, particularly as this was their first social interaction with their new neighbours.

Just take a deep breath, she thought. Surely Rae's parents will correct his rebellion. But no,

Handel merely took a seat next to his son and started a cheery conversation with Christian, who was standing behind Annabelle's seat.

"Hey, Christian, what sports do you like to play?" he asked with a huge smile.

Five-year-old Christian moved slightly towards Handel. He liked this man with the long hair and smiley face. He seemed to ooze warmth and comfort.

"I love T-ball and swimming."

"Oh, awesome, you'll have to come down the beach with us. I can teach you how to surf. We all surf. Have you ever tried?"

"No, but I would like to!"

Primrose's fears were all met at once. Surfing, smoking, drinking - the path to downward destruction of all mankind! Her mind began spinning even faster.

Rae started to chat quietly to Annabelle.

"I do free movement and yoga. I'll be looking for classes around here. Would you be interested?"

Annabelle smiled nervously, trying to avoid her mother's eyes, which she knew would be full of judgement.

Handel cracked opened his beer and gestured for Cee to come and jump on his knee. He embraced his young daughter with a big cuddle, saying to her "You'll be able to hit a ball with Christian." He winked at the young boy. "She has a mean arm!"

Cee giggled. "I can run like the wind, too!"

No modesty here, thought Primrose. They speak their minds.

Sunnie turned to Primrose, saying she needed to enrol her children in school.

"Do Annabelle and Christian go to the local schools?"

"No, they are both at the Christian College. We wish for their education to be a continuation of our home teachings."

Sunnie smiled. "Oh OK, maybe I'll look at enrolling Rae and Cee there, too. We want them to be open to all new experiences the city has to offer. They have had little religious exposure; maybe it would be nice for them to learn about faith while we are living here. We want them to be educated to understand that while religion has been at the root of war, racism and bigotry, its underlying morals are good. Love and kindness are what makes for a good family and peaceful world."

The discussion halted. There was silence as Primrose tried to process what she had just heard come out of this woman's mouth - and in such a pleasant tone. She seemed to be desecrating their religious beliefs while simply stating it as fact, without malice or confrontation.

Sunnie continued. "We want our kids to make decisions for themselves and not be brainwashed, and for that they need to be educated about all kinds of things, including different religions. Without education, we breed ignorance. We are not opposed to religion, we just choose not to follow it through traditional and formal ways."

Primrose could not believe what she was hearing. *Is this discussion really happening?*

To her, religion was a way of life, of living by example, not a topic of conversation in social settings. *I can clearly see you have no understanding,* she thought. She felt challenged by someone who appeared to have no qualms of expressing her thoughts and laying them on the line.

Handel broke the silence, addressing George. "Would you like a beer?"

George said he did not drink. "Abstaining from drinking, smoking, dancing and gambling are all part of our strong faith."

"Oh, gosh. That's a bit different, isn't it? Would you prefer if I didn't?" Handel looked at Sunnie and they seemed to share a moment.

"Actually, I would prefer if you didn't. If you don't mind." George was firm but polite.

Neither Rae nor Cee seemed bothered by the discussion and seemed open to what was being offered to them.

"Wearing a school uniform may restrict my style a bit, but I am open to change for a short period to compare it to my own values," Rae stated confidently.

"At home we try to wear simple clothing that's sustainable and kind to the planet as well as allowing freedom of expression – that's how we look on life. Everyone may not look the same or be painted with the same brush, but we are all linked together in a way that begins and ends in the same place. We respect everyone; their beliefs and their journey, as we try to make the world a more beautiful place - just like the colours of a rainbow. We should respect the world we live in and live in a way that sustains it, as we never want to lose the rainbow. There's no place for hatred, violence, racism, aggression or a closed mind in our world. Our family mantra is *'if you can't make someone's day a little brighter each day, you should try just that little bit harder'*.

Rae was on a roll now. "Mistakes are okay if you learn from them - without failure you will never strive to work harder. If you need a bit of nature's help - take it. Breathe the air, swim in the ocean, walk with your thoughts and organise them as you go. Don't let magazines, television or even your gender define who you are and where you are going. Don't conform to rules that have absolutely no reason - why can't boys wear their hair long? Who says boys can't dance? Girls can have careers too - girls can lead the world! And men can be the nurturers if they choose."

Rae's comments were all said with sincerity and thought, without aggression. He didn't sound controlling, just passionate. His comments clearly reflected the way he lived, and indicated how he had been influenced in a positive, free-thinking manner by his parents.

Primrose sat and listened to this young man, who had contributed some wise words to the conversation. *I like how this young man thinks,* she thought. Maybe, just maybe, our lives have restricted our children's own decision-making. They only know one way and that is the way of God, which will give them a good path to follow. But is it the only path? We have so many rules. I know children need boundaries – but have we built walls around them without doors?

Sunnie got up to help Primrose in the kitchen. She passed Cee and Christian, who were having a discussion in the sandpit that Christian seemed to be dominating. Sunnie stopped for a moment to listen. Christian was telling Cee that girls can't play ball with the boys. "You're not strong enough," his five-year-old voice chimed out. "You should go play with your dolls."

"I'm strong," remonstrated Cee. "I can do both. We can both play dollies. You can wash and feed the baby until I get home from work."

Little Christian objected. "I don't want to wash the baby; I want to go to work. You can wash the baby and feed him."

Cee looked at him. "Well this game won't work unless we both do different things. It's about sharing, and you are not being very nice."

Christian came around. "OK, I'll wash the baby if you show me what to do."

Both children were smiling. Confrontation had been avoided. No one was right and no one was wrong. It simply was the way it was. *If only everyone could learn a little compromise, the world would be a better place,* Sunnie thought. Why do we think that only one way – our way - is the right way? Yes, we had chosen to raise our children in the country and give them a voice of their own. That alone won't stop conflict, but it would hopefully help them to resolve it through wisdom and tolerance and the freedom to express it.

George was engaged talking to Handel. "Children pick up on our views at a young age. I have always felt that I need to teach, leading by example. Our roles in our home are very clear. I am the head of the household and it is my responsibility to provide a good home for my family. Strong Christian values are our guide. We want love, boundaries, and to follow the rules taught to us by our parents and there's before."

Sunnie's brain was working in overdrive. She decided to listen and not pass judgement, as it was not her place. In this instance, silence was best. She believed that children could teach adults valuable lessons if we would only stop and listen. It is easy to hear where they learn most of their conversation from. We are the ones that confuse them at times. Life only becomes complicated when we make it. It takes insight and a willing mind to change our taught perspectives. We must be careful we don't impose our views upon their malleable minds and allow them to have opinions of their own. What worked a decade ago is not necessarily relevant to society today. *Listen to my head, it sounds like a psychology book.* She laughed to herself.

Acceptance of others is why they had decided to move to the city. To learn another way of life, open other windows. As that happens, we will then have the ability to filter what we agree with and what we don't. If we don't give ourselves knowledge, we won't have the tools to pass judgement.

The rest of the evening passed uneventfully. The stars were high and a chill was setting in when Sunnie looked to Handel with that knowing glance again, and he made to get up.

"Well, we must be getting home to our packing boxes. Thanks for inviting us over. I'm sure we will be seeing much more of you as we settle in. You have a great family, and it's certainly neighbourly of you to welcome us with open arms."

He grabbed George into a bear hug and gave him a strong friendly thump on the back. George recoiled but quickly regained his composure.

"Lovely to have you all. Anything we can do to help you settle in, just let us know."

"Great! Maybe we'll see you all in the morning for a day of surf and fun. Look forward to seeing you all in your bathers!" He winked at Primrose, who immediately blushed bright red.

Christian and Annabelle said polite goodbyes, while Cee and Rae gave each of them a huge bear hug, beaming at their new friends. Primrose was again shocked by their directness, their warmth and sincerity. So unlike their usual friends!

The 'rainbow' family gathered themselves and left for their new home next door, laughing and chatting with each other about their day. Rae and Cee were glowing with praise about Annabelle and Christian, and they all looked forward to new adventures with the family they already considered friends.

They hadn't realised yet that the two families were worlds apart.

ANNABELLE

Christian and Annabelle were getting ready for bed. They each had similar routines: they would read quietly before their parents would come in to wish them goodnight. This night was a little different. Primrose sat on the edge of her daughter's bed and began speaking quietly; in Christian's room, George did the same. They gave each child the message they had rehearsed together.

Annabelle was not expecting what she heard from her mother. "Now Annabelle, we respect your friendship with our new neighbours, but we would also like you to make sure your friendship slowly imparts on them the knowledge of our Christian ways. Life is about rules and standards as you know."

Annabelle stayed quiet. *This is the way of our family*, she thought: *listen, obey and follow the rules. Do not question and do not speak back.*

"Life as they live it leaves them open to disaster and heartbreak," continued her mother.

"To open yourself to so many different views leads to confusion and may lead you down the path of destruction. So with your common sense and ways of God you can set an example. If you find yourself disturbed in any way, simply distance yourself from the friendship. Choosing your friends is very important."

Annabelle listened politely, nodding when appropriate and having little to say in response. Her mind had wandered elsewhere. She loved Rae's bright eyes, questioning mind and indifference to society's norms. He was happy with who he was, he was open to others, and he genuinely seemed happy.

Oh, how appealing this all seemed to her! Why do all the rules make life seem so rigid? Give of yourself to others. Always give 100 percent. I am sixteen! Surely life has to include *some* fun! I think with a Rae in my life the sun may shine again, she thought with a smile.

SATURDAY MORNING

Handel woke to the sun peeping through the open window. He could already feel the promise of another warm summer's day - a great reason to get up early.

He heard movement in the kitchen and the light banter of Rae and Cee. *Life's good*, he thought. This city move was the right thing to do. Despite powerful memories of green rolling hills falling into the sea, he was ready to paint new pictures with equal beauty. *It's all in how you look at the world*, he reminded himself.

Handel knew everything happens for a reason. He would never stop believing that life's path always gives us a lesson, no matter how difficult it might be at the time to understand. He and Sunnie had been sheltering their children from one particular truth. When the time was right, he would share it with them. But today, he would slip silently from the house to keep his early appointment at the hospital, to follow up on some worrying blood tests he'd had done in the country. This was the real reason Handel and Sunnie had decided to bring the family to the city. But neither of the children needed to be worried now as to where this illness may lead. As far as they were concerned, they were here to expand their life experiences.

Rae and Cee were keen to get down to the beach. Rae was waxing his board on the front lawn when he heard a voice call out his name. He looked up to see Annabelle walking towards him, all ready to join them on a day to the beach. She looked fresh but reserved. He smiled, pleased to see her out so bright and early. Obviously keen, which was a good sign.

Annabelle looked down on this refreshing, natural-looking boy with his wide grin and suddenly felt so overwhelmed. She really had to contain herself to resist spilling all her feelings out so that he did not run a mile. *I am really not his type*, she thought. He is so free and easy, and I am so controlled and reserved. How is a friendship even possible?

"Hi Annabelle." Rae sprung to his feet and gave her his usual bear hug. "I'm just getting the board ready for you. Dad will be back shortly from an appointment."

The van rolled round the corner at that very moment, pulling into the driveway with a rattle. Handel swung his arm out the window with a wild wave and a laugh, yelling to everyone to get a wriggle on.

Sunnie came out, closing the door behind her. "Come on Cee, let's go see if Christian is ready for our day at the beach."

She smiled at Handel, trying to gauge his expression, but his wide grin gave nothing away. This was a day to get out enjoy the sun and the sand and rejoice at them all being together, breathing in the sea air, sand between their toes, salt stiffening their hair and warm skin diving into cool freedom.

Primrose appeared with Christian, looking concerned.

"Sorry Sunnie, I am really not feeling the best this morning. So maybe Christian should stay with me. He can't swim and I don't want to spoil your day."

"Don't be silly, he will be no trouble at all. He will keep Cee company, which will make it easier on me." Primrose felt flustered and compromised but everyone was looking at her expectantly – especially Christian. "Well ... in that case – thank you."

They all piled into the van and once everyone was belted in, off they set. Handel turned on the radio. *Are you going to Scarborough Fair* sang out. The Brooks family began to sing. Wow! It was heavenly. Annabelle was shocked. The family's voices harmonised with Simon and Garfunkel as if they were all one. It was just so natural. *I love being included into this family,* she thought. It was easy, and fun. She realised she missed that. With Christian swaying beside her, she began to hum, and the drive to the beach melted into the music and blended with the warmth of this stunning day. *This was what a family should feel like.*

PRIMROSE

Back at home, George and Primrose were having a heated discussion. George's voice was raised as he spoke to his wife with aggression and control.

"Why would you not check with me first? We have only just met these people and to me, on first impressions, they do not seem the type you would trust your five-year-old son with after one meeting. Their appearance alone screams alarm bells. Their clothes are a mismatch, their hair is unkempt, and they drive an old van painted with the colours of a rainbow. Where is your brain?"

Tears fell silently down Primrose's face. Inside, she was shaking. She felt nauseated and was not in the mood to listen to George's unnecessary judgements and harsh words. She needed to lie down. As she turned away, she felt George grab her shoulder. He flung her around to face him.

"What the devil is wrong with you, woman? You know that I am the head of the household, and if I am here, I should make all the decisions regarding what the family is doing. Especially on the weekends, when it is family time. We were all supposed to go together to Saturday prayers, not offload our children onto a family we hardly know. Get out of my sight before I do something I regret."

Primrose went to her room and quietly closed the door behind her. She lay down and closed her eyes to the world, a world that she was starting to question.

THE BEACH

The van pulled into the parking bay and came to a standstill, brakes squealing. Umbrellas of every colour dotted the sand; towels were laid about randomly and children's squeals of delight rang out in the still heat.

Everyone spilled noisily out and ran off to find a space to call their own for the day. Sunnie, Christian and Cee took their buckets and spades to the water's edge for a sandcastle competition. Rae grabbed his board from the top of the van and followed them onto the sand. Annabelle watched as he peeled off his shirt and pulled on his wet suit. *Wow*, she thought. *He is simply perfect in every way - and he is going to teach me to surf!*

"Right, a few tips on land before we hit the water," Rae began. "It's all in the legs. So, from laying down flat you need to master getting to your feet and in the right stance in the one movement. Let's have a go."

Thank goodness her one-piece costume should hold up in the surf, thought Annabelle. The last thing she wanted was to spill out while she showed off her lack of surfing skills! *Concentrate on what he is saying, or you really will look like a fool.*

After a quick practice run on the sand, Rae said it was time to hit the water, and they paddled out to the break and faced the beach. Behind her, Annabelle could hear the waves approaching. The rumbling white foam threatened to engulf her and her board at any moment.

"Paddle!" she heard Rae roar. She paddled with a fury, looking back briefly to allow the force to propel her towards the beach. She struggled with all her might to lift her legs up and into position on the wobbling board. She kneeled, sprung to her feet as Rae had shown her – and overbalanced. She felt herself falling, feeling the rope pull on her ankle as she was rolled over and over in the turbulent white water. She tried to look up, through her hair, through the sand and the seawater, to the sky. After a few seconds - which felt like hours – Annabelle broke the surface, spluttering. She was still out of her depth, so she let the board drag her towards the shore until her feet hit the shifting sand. Rae appeared beside her, smiling and encouraging.

"That was great! Have another go!"

But Annabelle's pride was broken. She was a natural at most of the traditional sports like netball, softball and swimming. But this was different! It was not going to be as easy as it looked. But her natural determination took over. After a wait for the next set, a heavy whitewash with a good push set her on her way. She wobbled as she got to her feet but managed to hold her balance and she was off. The feeling was amazing. As the wave propelled her towards the shore with the wind in her face and the sun on her back, Annabelle felt a sense of freedom she had never experienced before. *Wow, I love this!* She heard a huge whoop as Rae shared her joy.

Back at the water's edge, Sunnie and Handel sat making sandcastles with the two little ones. Handel seemed a little distant and even though his voice was light-hearted, Sunnie could see the worry in his eyes. They hadn't had a chance to discuss his doctor's appointment, but Sunnie could tell he wanted to forget it for the moment, and just enjoy the day. Sunnie bided her time, not wanting to dampen the mood.

Saltwater, heat and family permeated Sunnie. She keenly felt that this was living: it was about the day, but she knew they were also all heading towards their destiny. *In the end it all comes down to how we live our lives each and every day,* she thought, looking at Handel. *Until one day it will be our last. Not just for one but for all of us. Don't lose sight of today.*

She became present in the moment again: sandcastles with moats, the deeper the better!

"Whoa, here comes a huge wave guys, this should fill the moat!" Water spilled into the trench and the little ones began to paddle in the water. As the water soaked into the sand, buckets and spades worked overtime in preparation for the next big wave. The wind was gentle, and the day was getting warmer by the minute. Despite being lathered in sunscreen, Sunnie could feel the sun penetrating and decided to move Cee and Christian into the shade of the umbrella. She didn't want to take Christian home burned and dehydrated.

"Ok guys, who is up for an ice cream and a drink? Thongs on and let's go!"

Life doesn't get much easier than this, she thought. No one was over-thinking the day, no one was thanking the guy above us all the time for giving us this beautiful day, everyone was just living it like there was no tomorrow. That is what made it special. Nothing complicated.

Yet for Annabelle and Christian, life had never been this free and easy. There had to be an agenda to everything and a blessing for every happiness or good fortune. They must be grateful to God that they had this life, be thankful every moment and remember not everyone is as fortunate as those who follow God.

We are all aware of how lucky we are. To be born in a country where everyone has a voice. Where everyone has the right to an education, access to health care, and welfare payments if times get tough. Everyone is worthy of these things, despite their background and beliefs. Yet to be constantly reminded and instructed to make yourself acknowledge these things can also make you a little twisted. Annabelle was becoming more aware and realising she had a conscience and a mind of her own. Her parents' views were not the only ones that mattered.

Right in this very moment, though, a choc mint ice cream was being devoured in the most idyllic situation she had ever found herself in. Rae was beside her and she was surrounded by a family that laughed and seemed to love life for just what it was.

Christian was sitting beside Cee and giggling like she had never heard before. Handel seemed just slightly distracted, but Sunnie was engaged with them all, genuinely loving this simple moment with her family and quickly helping the little ones manage their ice creams as they melted as fast as they were being licked.

Annabelle could just picture her mother stressing in this moment, trying to control every little drip of ice cream, wiping Christian's hands and face repeatedly and hurrying him to eat up or the whole thing would end up on his bathers. *So bloody wha*t was the attitude the Brooks had - mess was part of the fun. *I love it,* thought Annabelle. The Brooks seemed to just look on the sunny side of life, just as their mother's name depicted.

Ice creams devoured, it was time for some more surfing lessons. A few more nose dives and tumbles on the ocean floor would complete a near-perfect day.

Sunnie glanced over at Handel. He was sitting with his face down in a paper napkin that was fast filling with blood. She passed him a few more napkins.

"It's OK guys, just a nosebleed from the heat," she explained to the others. "Rae and Annabelle, you go on and I will stay here with the young ones." Both Sunnie and Handel were very matter of fact about it, so everyone went on with their plans. Not a biggie - simply a blood nose from the heat.

The surf was rolling in. Rae and Annabelle paddled out to the first small sets. Rae stood behind Annabelle to give her a bit of a push to gather momentum on the whitewash. Quickly she got to her feet, put her front foot forward and she was up. Her lithe body stood like a wobbly fawn, then settled. She stood firmly, feeling the wind hit her face. A feeling of freedom took over her whole body. The power of the swell pushed her forward and she thought *this is how I want to live.* At one with the world and all it has to offer without the complications of modern technology and the fast pace and the heavy burdens we place upon ourselves. Here, time slipped effortlessly by as she became one with nature. *This is my happy place.* Then she lost her balance and once more kissed the ocean's bottom. Well, that's just another metaphor for life, she thought, we have to take the highs with the lows. When we get knocked down, we get back up and don't wallow in tears. Annabelle's thoughts helped her resurface with a smile.

As the next wave started rolling into shore, she watched a surfer slide down its face and then manoeuvre back to the lip of the wave. Gliding along as it propelled him into his own world of freedom; escaping into one of the many gifts nature allows us to enjoy, if we only take the time to escape from the modern chaos we have created for ourselves. Technology would feed us twenty-four hours a day if we let it, stimulating us and overfeeding our anxieties, its endless rhythm putting pressure on us to live and look a certain way. Whereas nature only serves us when the conditions are right. So when the waves are perfect, we learn to appreciate them in the moment they create. Our minds become relaxed and calm as we settle into the rhythm of the ebb and flow of the sea.

I choose the wave, Annabelle thought quietly to herself.

Slowly and inevitably the sun crept towards the horizon. Everyone was feeling sated and a little parched from a day of fun, sun and surf. The Brooks and Christian and Annabelle strolled up to the colourful van. The drive home was a little quieter: music played gently in the background and the family quietly hummed or sang as they journeyed towards home. The silence was natural, not awkward and tense like so many of the silences experienced in the Robins' family home.

They pulled into the driveway. The Robins children thanked everyone and walked quietly next door for the next part of their day – for Annabelle, that meant dinner, prayers, quiet retrospection, and the constant reminder of how lucky she was to be alive. Praise be to God.

Primrose greeted her children at the front door, looking a little brighter and healthier than she felt. She had dinner on the table already, and as the family sat down, they held hands and George said grace. After giving thanks to the Lord, they ate in silence until George – who as head of the family was the instigator of all conversations – spoke to his children.

"I hope you remembered your manners today and did not speak out of turn."

Christian and Annabelle both said they had been well behaved. There were no questions as to what they did or whether it was fun. After a solemn dinner, it was time for the usual routine.

"Annabelle, you have some preparation for school. Christian, to bed."

Primrose spoke firmly, but there was tension in her voice.

RAE

The early morning sun peeped into the window of the bustling kitchen. The kettle sang out, the toast lurched out of the toaster, and conversation was bouncing off the walls. It was Monday - the first weekday of Rae's new city life, and Sunnie was taking him to get enrolled at college.

Rae had always been up with the birds. In the country, he would have done a day's work in the paddocks before hitting the schoolbooks, with his mother quietly bustling in the background. Life had been their schooling. They had seen birth firsthand through their horses, chickens and sheep. Nature had taught them so much. The ocean had been their playground. Now city life was to be their new experience.

Rae and Sunnie arrived at the college in the beat-up van. With her usual enthusiasm and energy, Sunnie leapt out of the van with a wide grin and, with her arm casually over Rae's shoulder, they entered the admin building together. Rae felt quite at ease, despite the new environment.

The school secretary greeted them and ushered them into the principal's office, where Mr Derwood asked them both to be seated. He handed them a brochure on the school, and its mission and school codes, asking Rae where he had been to school previously.

Rae smiled and said he had never been to school. He had always been home-schooled: life was his teacher, and his lessons took place at the beach and on the farm.

Mr Derwood stated that he would need to do some assessments to check that Rae had the right grounding to enter his year level.

"What are your goals and aspirations, Rae?" he asked.

"Just to do something I am passionate about, that makes a difference to not only myself but to others."

Mr Derwood was impressed. The young man spoke confidently, had presence and seemed to have a good outlook on life. He turned to Sunnie.

"Mrs Brooks, I can see from first impressions that your son is a fine young man with a lovely outlook on life. We would be lucky to have him as part of our school community. After his assessments we will give you his timetable and homeroom. The uniform shop is open now. We look forward to seeing you soon."

Annabelle was waiting outside the administration building. Rae gave her the thumbs up and a huge bear hug. The girls with her glanced at each other in shocked horror. Who was this new face, with hair to his shoulders and floppy clothes embracing their friend? They'd never even seen Annabelle look sideways at boys. She had some explaining!

"See you tomorrow, Annabelle." Rae gave her the biggest smile and whistled as he walked away, with his mother close by his side.

"Who was that!" "He is like no boy *I* have ever seen around here before!" "*I* think he looks like he comes from the planet of the apes!" Annabelle's friends cried in unison. "Get a haircut and a job, my dad would say," piped up Eloise.

"Well," Annabelle said, "he has moved in next door and he will be starting school here tomorrow. He is one of the nicest boys I have ever met. He has never been to school - he's been home-schooled and spent most of his life surfing and exploring the bush. He's never lived in the city before. We had them to dinner and the way they live life and explain things is like nothing I have ever known. I like him and his family a lot."

At the uniform shop, Rae felt his first doubts. This was a new experience. Pants, shirt, tie, blazer, socks, shoes. The school badge. *Woah* thought Rae. *I feel branded. Logos and ties that choke me in more ways than one. How can I do this?*

"Mum, this is not me. I am now having a few doubts about city life. You know I would rather not wear shoes. I feel that someone is telling me how I should dress and conform. This is reflecting someone else's life. This goes against everything you have taught me. I want to be free to express myself and not become someone that blends with the majority. I have no religious views and I definitely do not wish to have my life dictated to by others and their opinions."

His mother responded gently. "Rae, we also did not raise you to criticise or take a negative approach to others' different lifestyles. It's the way you look at the whole experience. It's not forever, it's just for now. Our job is to bring you up to be open-minded, and this will show you how a lot of people choose to live their lives. It can't all be bad, as this is the way most city children are educated. If you don't experience things for yourself, how are you supposed to make an informed decision as to whether it is right or wrong?

"The uniform will be something you will get used to, and you can stand out in other ways. Your strength of character and how you relate to others are your trademarks while you are at school. Contribute to school life, find where your interests lie and seize every opportunity to learn from people who have so much to teach. In the country you didn't have the variety of subjects or the competition you will have at this school. Don't be judge and juror until you have walked the walk, then you can talk the talk. OK?"

The next morning Rae put on his uniform and tied his long locks into a neat bundle at the base of his neck. He looked in the mirror and saw the face of conformity. His mother's words echoed in his mind, and he quickly stepped away from the mirror ready to live his new life, without negative reflection or expectations. Seize the opportunity. Take the positive and let it lead you to the path of endless growth. Yep, that's the way to look at it.

He ate breakfast, and after a warm embrace for each of his parents he left the house to meet Annabelle to walk to school.

Primrose answered the door and was shocked to see Rae looking very neat and well-groomed in his new uniform. "My goodness Rae. How lovely to see you looking so smart. You will love this school. It will be the making of a new young man with strong Christian values."

Rae smiled politely and nodded. *What a load of bull*, he thought.

Annabelle appeared and he realised all was not so bad. She pecked her mother on the cheek and swept them both quickly out of the house.

"How are you feeling?" she asked him. "A little uncomfortable to be honest. Not my usual daily dress code."

He laughed easily and Annabelle was once again drawn in by his warmth and honesty.

As they strolled the conversation flowed easily. Nothing was forced or awkward. Not like our home, Annabelle thought. Where every word was analysed and every discussion had to have meaning. Not one day went by without thanking the Lord for absolutely every little thing and putting others down for not following the way of God. She understood that to live a wholesome life is good, yet being reminded of it every second of the day became tiresome. She felt as though she had to think before every word she spoke. It was easier to say nothing and stay in her room.

For her, the Brooks' easy banter and exuberance for life meant freedom – and she wanted more of it.

SCHOOL

At the school gates they parted ways. Rae went into the admin building, where he was given his timetable and directions to his first class. He arrived at the classroom quickly to find everyone was milling outside chatting noisily. It was like a flock of black cockatoos gathered in groups and incessantly squawking. The noise was loud and incessant.

He was a little overwhelmed with how they all huddled and were so engrossed in each other that no one noticed his approach. So, this was city life? No one takes the time to observe when something new is approaching? Are they all too engrossed in their own little worlds? Do I even want to be a part of this uniform, routine life? How do we stand out when we all conform? How do we allow our creative authentic selves to grow when our environment is structured to stifle our individuality? *If I dwell on this I am going to feel deflated and obsess on all that has been taken from me, instead of all that I may take from this new experience.* His mother's voice appeared in his head. *Take this opportunity and embrace all it has to offer. To avoid new experiences stifles and limits your outlook on life. We need to make comparisons to find what is right for us.*

The bell rang. He followed the group in, and was the last to enter the room. Everyone had taken their seats and he wandered to the last seat available. The teacher followed his every move and then glanced at his clipboard and greeted the room.

"Good morning, everyone. I would like to introduce a new member of our school community, Rae Brooks. I would like you all to make him feel welcome and introduce yourselves when you have the chance.

"Now, could you all bow your heads and give thanks to the Lord who has given us this beautiful day and be thankful for all the opportunities you have in your life."

A few minutes silence followed.

"Right, OK now, let's get on with the class. We will be discussing today how technology is of benefit in society. I would first like to hear from each one of you, about one benefit it has given to you personally. Let's start with you, Rae, and then perhaps you could please just briefly tell us where you have come from and a little about yourself. "

Rae got up, dazzling the class with his wide smile as he turned his head to sweep the room and take in everyone with a glance.

"Hi everyone. Technology has only just this week touched my life. The mobile phone I now own has given me the freedom of knowing that I may always be in touch with my parents should I need them, as well as to follow snapchat, Instagram and Facebook."

A few laughs erupted around the classroom.

"I come from a small country town around 400 kilometres from here on the southern coast. I lived on a farm property bordering the beautiful coastline with my parents and young sister. We lived a self-sustainable lifestyle; I was always home-schooled. I love to surf and fish, and I love music. Our only form of contact was face-to-face, and we got around the property on horseback.

"We never had electricity and lived on rainwater, so every drop of water was precious to us. I have also never used a computer, so I am not very 'hip' or happening or up with many of the benefits of technology today. It's a world that is foreign to me, but I'm sure I will understand it all a little more with time.

"It's nice to be here and I'm really looking forward to being a part of a school environment."

Rae had given each and everyone in the class a glance, a smile and what everyone needs, acknowledgement. Each and every face was transfixed with his introduction, male and female. He discriminated against nobody in that room, he was inclusive, and they all were feeling like he was their best mate already. Normally, people scanned the room and quickly made a judgement of who they might like and dislike. Not Rae. He had no reason to discriminate. His world had always been and always would be inclusive, non-judgemental and completely open and honest. Life was about living with the world, looking after each and every living thing in it, and making choices that made the world a better place. He understood his choices made an impact not only on other humans, but the ocean, the vegetation and other wildlife. We must all live in harmony. This group of city kids had grown up constantly bombarded by information from TV, radio, billboards and the internet. Their choices were so wide it was overwhelming. They had been taught God's way, and a good Christian education was a solid foundation for all their learning. But instead of actually following these teachings of kindness, forgiveness and acceptance, many became intolerant of others who weren't like them. Yet they will be given a doorway to heaven only if they follow the teachings of the church. So many rules to follow.

Where was the freedom of choice, the learning by experience and being taught that being different was good, it made you authentic? Rae was both puzzled and startled at the information the other kids were contributing. He realised again how different his life had been because of his parents' choices. Was it better, or just different? He decided at this moment to say it was simply different. *I will wait till I have lived with both before I judge.* Despite his freedoms, he had had no influence over how he lived: his parents had made a life choice they felt would benefit them all. Just as the parents of these children had decided what was best for them. It made him understand that life is complex, and he had a lot to learn.

The bell rang and everyone hustled to get to the next class. A boy next to Rae asked him what his next class was. It was the same as his, so they headed off together. Most of the group appeared to be moving in the same direction. It was Religious Education. A first for Rae. *Open yourself to new ways of thinking. Nothing is without merit. Take what you can from the information and throw away what you feel is of no use.*

The class filed in quietly and orderly and went directly to their assigned seats. One seat remained close to the teacher, Pastor Dan Johns, better known as Pastor Dan. Rae, sat himself down discreetly. A heading was marked in bold letters on the board: 'The relevance of Christianity in today's world.'

"Today's discussion is listed above," Pastor Dan spoke. "Who would like to start us off today?"

A brooding, dark-haired girl put her hand in the air. Pastor Dan nodded at her. She stood and started to speak clearly and confidently.

"In today's world we need Christianity more than anything. From the media, we all are aware of those suffering, be it from natural disasters or civil war. To turn a blind eye is un-Christian. We can all make a difference, even if in only a small way. If we look to having an opinion and standing together, we have a louder voice that can help those in need. If no one speaks up for injustice, then those that lead others into damnation will do so with ease."

"Thank you Dreya." Pastor Dan motioned to a boy whose arm was raised. "Thomas?"

Thomas stood and spoke quietly. "I think those that believe God has a hand in everything have to truthfully say many questions remain unanswered. Why would a God that is good allow so many to suffer and create a world that provides an abundance to some and denies many the human basics of water and shelter?"

As he sat down, another arm shot up. Ruth, a tiny blonde girl with pigtails, stood to speak.

"I would like to try and answer Thomas. Many things in life seem unjust, but enduring pain and suffering gives us insight and we hopefully learn from our mistakes. War, though, is suffered by those who did not create the problem.

"Young children starve and become homeless, and families are left with nothing. Many wish to leave their homeland to seek a better life. We have refugees arriving on our shores, and as Christians, we should give them back their dignity. Governments concerned more about budgets and statistics have little time to really see the reality. Compassion has no monetary value; therefore, it is way down the list. Human stories are lost.

"We are never too young to listen to the stories of others, and to realise our lives are created unequal, impacted by the decisions of others. We have little control over where we are born and to whom we are born. Yet we do have the power to direct ourselves out of situations if we take the path that sometimes may not be the easiest."

The class was silent as they realised what Ruth was saying. All this was happening right now, close to them. Yet they went about their lives like no one else existed, absorbed in the daily dramas about boyfriends and girlfriends, and relationship breakdowns and who was on Instagram.

Rae sat, listened and contemplated how each of these students listened to others, and seemed to have real compassion for others.

These adolescents were being taught to care about others. That cannot be a bad thing. So many teenagers simply put themselves first and believed the world owed them everything.

If this was religion, it couldn't be all that bad. He had had no religious teaching from his parents, as they believed we are part of a universe that is much larger than us and we must protect it to allow us to live in harmony. To Rae, religion seemed to have a similar outcome if the rules were followed: treat each and every one with humanity. Unfortunately, though, with any group - be it religious, political or simply a gathering of quilters - the human dynamics can make for trouble. As we splinter off and divide into smaller groups, our beliefs can turn into disagreements with other groups, upsetting what was a harmonious community. It happens in all walks of life.

Rae decided he would have to listen a little more to understand this Christian life. He was prepared to have an open mind. For as his mother said, an open mind links closely to an open heart, and with an open heart, love will sustain you much longer than hatred ever could. Start each day with an open mind and an open heart and you will learn and live, gaining an abundance of free-spirited positive energy. His way was to breathe in deep, then breathe out just as deeply and think about life. It needs to be no more complicated than you make it. So from now on, when he chose to quietly meditate and contemplate life, he would try and think about God. It seemed a little more complex than simply existing with nature, and it appears to have caused conflict for many, but with a little more thought and understanding it may be something he could understand and embrace. *Annabelle seems to live by the rules quite rigidly, and she is lovely,* he thought to himself.

Meanwhile, Annabelle was watching Rae and thinking how can he be so perfect? He has freedom, a family that loves him and allows him to think for himself, respecting his opinion. In her home, life was lived by the clock, by the rules and by following

God's teachings, day in and day out. It was restrictive and tiresome and was making her resent her parents.

She was totally distracted by Rae and did not listen to a word spoken in class. The bell rang and she walked out in a dream. There must be more than church and living by the rules it applies. She wanted to become a part of Rae's family and live with freedom and choices. Rae sidled up beside her and asked if she was heading straight home after school.

"Yes," she replied. "What about you?"

"I may stop off at the shops for a while and then stroll down to the river. You want to come?"

'Um ... no, I can't, I have to get home and help prepare the meal, then I have to go to Bible reading class. Then it's straight home."

"Maybe another time then." He smiled as he headed over the road, where he bumped into a group of classmates heading in the same direction.

Annabelle's pulse began to race, and she tried to regain control of her breathing. She knew this feeling well. Suddenly her chest would tighten and her head would become light. She stopped and tried to remain calm. She felt a moment of doom as the tears sprung to her eyes. This overwhelming emotion was not something new to her. She tried hard to tackle it without panicking. It had been happening more and more lately. As she started to feel she could breathe again, she slowly continued her walk home. A darkness came over her and she felt immense sadness as she realised she would never be able to live with the freedom Rae was so used to. Why did her parents place so much importance on living by rules? She would not mind so much if they were just a little less rigid.

Annabelle arrived home, unlocked the front door and headed straight to the kitchen. The instructions were out for what she must prepare for dinner, along with a plate of biscuits to take to

Bible class. A note lay neatly beside the instructions telling her not to forget to be thankful and praise God.

She sighed, got on with the job at hand, then left for Bible class. Today the class spoke of acceptance, of living in a way that God approved, of loving our family and a life serving God and others. All good things, but somehow, at this moment, none of it was adding up to Annabelle. It wasn't enough. Her father and mother gave her no voice. They judged others and were not accepting of anyone with a different outlook on life. They also seriously restricted her personal space!

Somehow, she needed to ease out of these boundaries and start experiencing life. Surely having a boyfriend, or a drink here or there, wouldn't mean I would end up in the fires of hell? She certainly meant to find out.

A DIAGNOSIS

Sunnie was in the kitchen listening to music while assembling a tofu salad, a glass of wine by her side. She was deep in thought.

Why would a beautiful world strike such a blow to a man so full of life and vitality in the peak of his life? Some things just can't be explained. Handel's blood results had shown a further increase in white cells. The news of his diagnosis was settling in, and they were realising some home truths. Their lives were about to change dramatically. As a family they had some challenges to face and conquer. How they did that and still enjoy their daily life was going to be a challenge. They would need great strength and unity in what would be a very testing time.

The arrival of Rae interrupted her thoughts. "Hi, my ray of sunshine! How was your day?"

"Mmm ... different from what I am used to. Yet I loved how it made me think about life in a different light. Allowing me to weigh up a few things. I find the thought of religion and God quite daunting, yet I can also see that to believe in something so much bigger than we are is maybe a lifeline to healing and strength. If I look at everyone and their different belief systems, I see a common thread - we all seem to like to group together with similarly minded people and support each other. That's a good thing, as long as we don't lose sight of others outside our group and become extreme in our ways of thinking. That's how wars start!"

"Wow, that's deep. Family dinner in fifteen - get yourselves cleaned up and we will eat outside. Your dad and I need to tell you and Cee about some things we need to face while we're living here in the city."

The family gathered outside as the sun settled over the western horizon. It was a lovely summer evening. The sky was ablaze with burnt-orange clouds and pink streaks, and the sun glowed red as it dropped to meet the sea and rest for the evening. A stunning end to the day.

Handel sat on the bench under the large willow tree with his guitar, strumming a tune and humming to himself. The birds quietened as dusk approached, and a stillness enveloped the Brooks' new surroundings. It was a perfect picture of harmony.

They all sat down around the table in the garden. Sunnie smiled and told everyone to dig in. They began to eat, and the usual chatter sounded out. Then Handel quietly turned to the children. His look was warm, but his eyes were moist.

"I have something to tell you both. We have had some news today that means our lives may change for a little while. We know we have asked you both to embrace some big changes of late. Change is something life expects of us now and then. If everything remained the same, we would never grow and learn how to live a bigger and better life. Sometimes the things that expect us to change the most, make us grow so much more than we realise at the time.

"I am facing one of those challenges right now. I've been told I must undergo some treatment to help me fight an illness that, unless I fight it with vigour, may beat me. You know I have always fought for what I believe in, and I will still do that. I believe I will be well again, so I want to keep fighting. But this time I can't do it alone. I have to fight this battle with some help from the doctors in the city. And I need all of you to help me, too. I will have good days and bad, but through it all I know we will have each other to laugh with and cry with.

"I've been diagnosed with leukaemia, a disease that has caused my body to over-produce one kind of cell. We have red and white cells; my white cells are malformed and multiplying, so they can't do their job of helping my body fight infection and keep things in balance.

Hopefully, I will find a bone marrow match, have a transfusion and recover fully. In the meantime, life will go on as usual, but I may need to spend a bit of time in the hospital. I may also be a little more tired than usual and will need to rest and sleep more. Life won't be as active for me."

Rae and Cee were silent, taking in their father's words.

"Why has this happened to us? Why is the world spinning and I am still? The answers are hidden in science. Yet I still have to-morrow, so let's take each day as we wake and be grateful for it. Together, we'll take one step at a time, side by side. Take my hand and when I stop to shed a tear, grab me and hold me close. Our hearts will get us back to a steady pace. As long as I hear that beat, I will continue to walk with you. The day my heart stops, re-member my spirit will leap from me to everyone I have touched, so that I will always be there if you search among yourselves.

"Be happy for today, and be grateful we have teams of doctors who will help me fight this battle. But the one thing I know will help me get through it is something not everyone is as fortunate to have - and that is you guys! We live by the rule that 'love is all we need.' So keep those smiles in your hearts and let's do this to-gether! Life is a rainbow. It's the colours in our life that shape us. In our darkest, stormiest times, what do we look for?"

The family held hands and responded together:

Rainbow with your many hues
Guide me through my day of blue

Storms darken skies above
Lighten it with coloured love.

Sunnie took over from Handel. "You know we've always looked to nature for the answers: natural medicines from plants, Vitamin D from the sun, or simply good food, clean, fresh air and salt on your skin from the ocean. Nature is free, and if you soak it up chances are you will remain healthy. It's all the chemicals and man-made substances that are causing us to have toxic build-ups within our bodies. It's largely a 'First World' problem. So here we are today having to treat a problem caused largely by toxicity, with toxic chemicals. Chemotherapy will be your father's life saver."

"We will beat this, guys," Handel said. "Just stay focused on being happy and loving and supportive of each other. We'll be going through this journey together. Along the way we will be shocked, angry, sad, reflective, and ultimately accepting of this challenge we are facing.

"But enough of my philosophies of life for tonight! We'll know more by the end of the week as to how my treatment will be progressing. In the meantime, concentrate your thoughts on the energy that will help us get through this challenge. Sleep tight my bundles of love, and we will tackle another day with courage tomorrow.

"And remember, your mum and I love you guys for ever and a day!"

SWEET DREAMS

Next door, as the night darkened, Primrose and George were having a heated discussion about their number one problem in life - their new neighbours.

"How can our world be tipped upside down so suddenly," whined Primrose.

As George got up from the kitchen table, he could feel the anger rising from his toes to form the words that spewed from his mouth. "I will not let others change my children's views. We have chosen a life that promotes respect and belief in God and his values."

He picked up his bible.

"It tells us in his book how we should live. If everyone simply chose their own value system, the world would go to hell! I think we need to monitor this situation closely. Our children need to respect us and what we wish for them."

He turned to Primrose. "I think you, as their mother, need to take a firmer hand. Speak to Sunshine and guide her to the light. Our path is the way all must walk, or the world is doomed. We will not tolerate our values being challenged so blatantly. If I don't see you making an effort to change their heathen influence on our children, I will be forced to punish you for your lazy ways and not following the Christian values God wills upon us all."

Primrose hung her head and averted her eyes from her husband's glare. She was feeling exhausted and extremely nauseated. She simply nodded her head, said she would do her best, and went to bed.

George took his usual position in his well-worn recliner and closed his eyes to pray that the morning would bring the answers to his new-found worries.

How can I change the world so that it follows what is right? he prayed. *The darkness surrounds those who choose not to follow the ways of the divine. Annabelle must follow my rules or I will have to stop her contact with this boy. I will not see her turn to these loose, unconventional ways that are destroying the progression of mankind. A firm hand and strict rules will stop this nonsense from going any further towards the path of destruction. Praise be to the Lord, who guides us and gives us what we need to survive and live in the right way until we give ourselves over in our final days on this earth.*

Darkness settled and slumber came to most. Yet footsteps still lightly pattered on the lino upstairs. Primrose could not sleep. Her nausea was increasing, and she could not ease her unsettled mind. Racing thoughts and comparisons consumed her. Annabelle was turning into a young woman and she could see her attraction to Rae was very real and growing. George had become so rigid in his way of thinking it was unnerving her. He was becoming more unreasonable every day, and her role as a wife was being tested. She knew she must obey and not question him, yet a swell of discontent was rising inside her. If she was perfectly honest with herself, her bare-chested neighbour, with his easy laugh and magnetic smile, was stirring feelings she thought were long dead. She felt like a character in a soapie reacting to the charming ways of the handsome hero. This was simply not her! And her faithful prayers were not helping her at all. Chaos seemed to be worming its way into her ordered existence.

Tears began to slide down Primrose's cheeks and she wept silently in the darkness. She was starting to lose respect for the life she had chosen. Where was she leading her children? Is there really a heaven or hell? Is life really that black and white? Does love exist in different forms? Can we only have one love and never love again? Her thoughts were profound but going around and round, getting her nowhere. Primrose had always followed the simple Christian rule of love thy husband. He was the head of the household and would protect and lead us where we need to go, with the guidance of God's will. But after tonight and the past few weeks, her thoughts were being challenged, turning her life upside down. *Tomorrow is another day*, she thought.

Eventually her mind calmed, and she returned quietly to bed. Sleep would take her to where her mind needed to go. She closed her eyes and fell into her private dreamland, where life played out in a very different way.

A windswept, bare-chested man walked past her. He reminded her of a large latte - smooth, strong and easy to take. Her mind's eye took in every inch of him as she slipped into a sinful place that made her feel absolutely delicious. A walk along the beach was an eyeful of pure delight, as half-naked bodies, lean and toned, ran past her. Hiding her eyes behind dark glasses, she brazenly stared at what she wickedly wished for. Jogging towards her was a man she could not take her eyes from. He had long golden hair and skin like warm caramel. Unlike the other runners, this man slowed down and stopped before her. Her heart raced and she could not help but stare. He had eyes that sparkled like the sea, and a smile that could wash away the world's problems. She felt like she was in a movie, or a glorious, sensual advertisement.

He spoke clearly, with a warm, rich tone. "Morning, gorgeous. How are we on this golden day? Have you the time to take in the sunshine and cool waters, and a man that tastes like chocolate, who is looking for something new and sweet in his life?"

Primrose liked what she saw and smiled bashfully at his melting words. Today it felt like something new was in the air. Life was about change and risk. He held out his hand and she took it with pleasure.

"My flower is waiting to bloom," she told him. "Your rays are warming parts of me I thought had frozen years ago. I am yours in any way you like. Take me now and take me to waters I have not swum in before. You are everything I have dreamed about and more."

Woah, where did those words come from! Even asleep, Primrose shocked herself.

I don't know, I don't care and please don't let my mind awaken and take from me what only exists in dreams.

In the man's eyes, Primrose could see kindness, escape, and the need to fill her desires. She was ready to take it all. She felt wonderful. Her arms and her heart opened as they slowly came together, swimming entwined in nakedness of both body and heart. A warmth started to rise from deep within Primrose that quickly became a fire that burned fast and furious. A sense of safety and security wrapped her up and tied them both with a huge ribbon. They were one huge present ready to be given to the world, surrounded by all the colours of the rainbow. She was swept into a surreal world; lifted to an emotional high that she had very rarely experienced.

Primrose gasped for air as reality smacked her in the face. George's voice was close, waking her with a start. "Get up, Primrose. It's time to get us organised."

Primrose lay still as she realised her dream was just that. A dream. As she sat up, her head spun. Nausea overwhelmed her. Slowly she got up to tackle her morning tasks and get her family ready to start their day.

CIRCLE OF LOVE

It was Handel's first day of treatment, and the Brooks' house was buzzing. Everyone was doing their best to get on with the morning routine and help each other out. Love and a helping hand, when done with a good heart, makes for another perfect day.

Before Handel and Sunnie set off out the door, they grabbed the kids and got into their 'circle of love' as they called it, and spoke together:

"May we all enjoy this day and take from it something we had not learned yesterday. May our love be our strength and help us conquer all our fears. Love you today, tomorrow and every day after that.".

"Rae, make sure you get your sister to school on time. Help her pack her lunch and bag. Maybe you could go next door and offer to walk Christian too."

Then they were off, leaving the kids to get to school under their own steam.

Rae knocked on Annabelle's front door. Inside, he could hear raised voices: George was yelling at Christian. It took a while for things to quieten, and after he knocked once more, Annabelle came to the door. She looked embarrassed.

"Sorry, we are in a bit of a mess this morning. Mum is feeling unwell and dad is trying to get Christian to hurry, with not much success."

Rae spoke with cheer in his voice. "Would you like to walk with me, and we can drop Cee and Christian on the way?"

Annabelle looked grateful and said she would just be five minutes if he would like to wait outside.

George was looking on unhappily as Christian hurriedly grabbed his lunchbox and bag and took Annabelle's hand. His father frightened him when he got this angry over simply not having his shirt buttoned correctly. He quietly said goodbye and Annabelle gave her father a small peck on the cheek.

Rae smiled brightly and started chatting as if he had heard nothing, and life was just going along on its merry way. He playfully grabbed Christian's shoulder. "Where's that gorgeous giggle of yours today? Cee said you are the funniest boy she has ever met!"

Christian's cheeky grin looked up at Rae. "How do all the oceans say hello to one another?" he asked. Rae, Cee and Annabelle smiled and shrugged. "They wave!" Christian shouted.

Their laughter sang out as they walked and jostled each other along the footpath. Annabelle smiled at Rae and was touched by his kindness and ability to change their sadness so easily. She was already forgetting how the day had started and the harsh words between her parents. It seemed to her that Rae had everything going right in his life. Laughter made everything that little bit easier.

Christian looked up at Rae, beaming with a cheeky grin, ready to tell him another of his lame jokes. Rae gave both him and Cee a gentle nudge and sent the little ones into school with a laugh.

Now Annabelle was alone with Rae. The banter and childish giggles stopped. Rae had a serious expression on his face. He turned to her with a concerned expression. "You OK?"

"Been better," Annabelle admitted. "There's just a bit of tension at home and I'm finding it all a bit difficult."

"Sorry to hear that, Annabelle. If you need someone to listen, I am always here. Life throws curve balls from time to time. What I've learned is a trouble shared is a trouble halved. So when you are ready, I am here. I have sturdy shoulders and a mouth that only speaks what will not hurt others. In other words, what you tell me will not go any further."

"Rae, thank you. I am so glad you have moved in next door. You are a breath of fresh air, scented with all the good things from this earth!"

He threw his arm around her shoulder and flashed her his infectious smile.

"Happy to help. Mum always says never think you are alone with your problems, as everyone is burdened with troubles. It is how we react to them that makes the difference. Worry about what you can control and let the other stuff sort itself out. Seems to work. Also breathe deeply and allow the spirit of the earth to fill you with good thoughts! And don't take life too seriously; we all end up in the same place eventually."

Annabelle simply smiled. *Yes, he's right. Let the parents resolve their own issues and just focus on living each day.* A day that had started out badly due to a controlling, angry father was slowly changing, as a gentle kindness replaced the anger. She felt lighter as she and Rae continued onto school with a skip in their step and laughter in their hearts.

GEORGE

Primrose was retching into the toilet as George whinged about how the kids have no organisation and Christian can barely dress himself. Then he turned his wrath on to her.

"What's up with you lately? All this feeling so unwell? You should rest properly so you can get on your feet quickly. This house needs you to get it running smoothly. There's been no discipline of late."

George left the house and went to work. He ran a large printing company that was a hive of activity, with 300 staff who all had something to question the boss about on a weekly basis. Some of the employees came from families that had worked for the business for generations. Many of them attended the same church each week, so George felt he had a huge responsibility to his staff, both morally and ethically.

Face value was extremely important to George. Each week his family fronted up to church, exemplars of model Christian citizens. There were no grounds for gossip about the Robins family!

George sat at his desk and focused on the day ahead. A message popped up on his computer screen, which he quickly read and then deleted. The day soon got hectic, and George was kept busy moving about between staff and meetings and phone calls. It was 6pm before he had time to glance at the clock.

Primrose's day continued as unpleasantly as it started. Her nausea was all-consuming, and she was finding it difficult to tackle simple household chores. If it continued, she might need to visit the doctor. George had really pushed her too far this time. Hiding the truth, joining with others who believed that by a Sunday visit to church, all their sins would be washed away. Well, this time it may not be so easy to hide. She was frustrated with herself for allowing herself to be swept away by a selfish need and not seeing how it could end up hurting those she loved the most, her children.

How could she judge others so harshly and then hide behind the church? Her handsome new neighbour was making it extremely difficult for her to mask what was becoming a habit – the dreams that she looked forward to at night. George had caught her glances, and she had copped the wrath of his anger. Only those under God's guidance, with roles within the church, have the power to test us and teach us the way to live, and if we choose not to follow, we will be judged by our Maker. But if her sickness was what she thought it may be, God and his leaders had made one almighty mistake.

Maybe the church's words that women are to be loved by the men who guide them was about to be tested by their little prayer group. Maybe their teaching had become a little *too* close.

Anyway, thought Primrose. A visit to the doctor was needed first.

CHAPTER

13

A JOURNEY BEGINS

Handel took a deep breath. Holding it, he gently repeated to himself - *peace, serenity and good health*. His thoughts were in order, his breath was calm, and he had his sense of humour intact. He smiled at the reception staff in the medical suite, and he was directed into a cubicle to change into his gown for the beginning of his chemotherapy.

So here we go. Sunnie would be here after the nurses had set up the infusion. She had wanted to visit the bookstore first to get some natural therapy books so they could tackle this journey head-on and together. She wanted the family to remain focused on the outcome and not on the grief. To enjoy each moment they had, and not get so consumed by the dread that they missed the opportunities given to them all in this precise moment. They had some tools to do this themselves, but some inspiration from others who had been on this journey would simply be another way of them caring for each other during this difficult time.

No one can tell you exactly how to react and how to love during this journey, but if we all show some understanding towards each other it will help.

For now, Sunnie realised Handel needed some space. Moments alone to digest what was happening, and time with the health professionals who could explain everything to him without her gazing over his shoulder and predicting his every reaction. Sometimes good intention can be smothering.

The collection of books on cancer was expansive. Holistic medicine, herbs, meditation, diet. Where did she start? It was all rather overwhelming. Then she saw a little hand-drawn book and the title: *A Child's Journey Through Treatment.* Sometimes the mind of a child sees things in a light that is uncomplicated. She flicked through and it caught both her eye and her heart. This was the book to start to lighten the road.

Sunnie briefly read the prologue written by the child's mother. It lifted her spirit and she realised this was just what she needed. This woman spoke from a place that resonated with Sunnie. There was both insight and humour, from a place of innocence not tainted by knowing too much or delving too deeply. People complicate situations as they get older and think too deeply. Yet a child lives in the moment and life teaches them something new every day. They are happy to take instruction from others and do not judge as quickly as most adults. The fear they know is only what they have been taught.

The book had an illustration on each page drawn by the nine-year-old who beat the demon. The title page was a drawing of a girl with a golden halo; there were dark clouds behind her and a rainbow over the entire background. She had no hair and her huge eyes sparkled like diamonds. She was smiling, yet a tear dropped from one sparkling eye. She was reaching out her hand to a doctor in a white coat. Her mother was by her side.

This set the place and journey of one little girl's battle with cancer. Sunnie began to read:

> It is easy to think we can take the scary side away by nurses not wearing a uniform, or a doctor wearing a clown suit. Yet the reality is, being sick *is* scary. No matter how the staff dress, no matter how the walls are painted. The un-

known always creates some fear. It is not how the staff look that the patient will remember, but how they made them feel.

It is not only your child that is experiencing the fear, but the whole family. The moment the staff begin the journey with your child and the family. the emotions begin.

I would like to share our journey to help others.

Wow, I love this. Sunnie walked to the front counter to pay. The girl behind the counter lifted her head and looked her straight in the eye.

"This is one of the most beautiful little books I have read this year," the girl said. "It will make you cry, yet will also give you moments where you smile and want to laugh out loud. I hope it helps whoever you are buying it for, and it gives them hope."

"Thank you, so do I," replied Sunnie, tucking the book under her arm and heading around the corner to start this challenge alongside her gorgeous man.

As she entered the medical suite, her stomach sank just that little bit, and a few butterflies started fluttering within her. Everything was new. A receptionist wearing a badge saying 'Evita' greeted her warmly, asking if she needed help. Sunnie spoke clearly. "My husband Handel is having his first treatment this morning." With a kind voice, Evita asked Sunnie to follow her. Sunnie's eyes swept the rooms as she passed. So many different people sitting reading, listening to music or simply just relaxing while chemicals dripped slowly into their bodies to begin the war on cancer.

Handel beamed when he saw her. She reached for his hand. "How's it going, handsome?"

"Feeling a bit queasy, but otherwise I am OK."

She sat down beside him and they both sat quietly, squeezing each other's hand. Sometimes words are just not necessary. Time passed by and the liquid slowly dropped into Handel's vein, taking on the fight for his life. As the last of the fluid entered, he was gripped by severe nausea, and his face paled as the nurse quickly passed him a kidney dish. He felt like death, and the fight he had within him this morning quickly dwindled as reality hit hard. A tear slid down and touched his lips. But the salt was not what he needed to taste; all his senses seemed heightened, and he reached for the kidney dish once more. The world spun and everything seemed to be wrenched from his insides.

This is one journey where I will need all my inner strength, Handel thought. *My mind will need to be powerful enough to overcome my physical weakness, otherwise this war will be lost very easily. I am not alone. Grant me strength, peace and serenity and may I only be dealt with what I can cope.*

Handel repeated the mantra over and over to help him overcome any other negativity that may squeeze its way in to his thoughts. Every time a sad thought entered his mind, he repeated the lines. Slowly he started to feel his strength return and the nausea pass.

When he opened his eyes, Sunnie was there. She smiled and quietly whispered, "I love you."

A nurse entered the room and asked how Handel was feeling.

"The nausea is still there, but my head has stopped spinning." She gave him a prescription for the nausea and an appointment card, urging Handel to call if he had any problems. As Handel and Sunnie walked out into the fresh afternoon, the cold air fuelled another bout of dizziness and nausea. All Handel wanted to do was get home, get comfortable and rest with those closest to him.

CHAPTER

14

LITTLE LIES

Prying eyes watched Sunnie and Handel holding each other close as they walked slowly into their home next door. *How supportive and close these two free-spirited lovers are.* A pang of jealousy hit Primrose. Life was becoming increasingly difficult to stomach in this household lately. The only part of her life that made her feel really alive was a secret, and had nothing to do with the way she presented herself to the world. When would harmony and peace become a natural part of her life, and not something she was constantly searching for from a higher perspective?

Primrose was feeling disgruntled with her life and starting to judge harshly those she loved the most. She realised she must stop looking outside for her own contentment and accept that if she wanted her world to change, she must start with herself. Anyway, her neighbours seemed to be getting something right when it came to love.

The window she looked out of gave her a clear view of everything she felt she did not have in her own life. As she saw George pull into the driveway, instead of skipping a beat, her heart began to drop into her stomach. Dinner, Bible studies and serious discussions loomed. George's heart was in the right place, but dealing with the rigidity of her Christian faith was starting to make her feel very uneasy - and even queasy a lot of the time. Constantly trying to live a consciously good life was becoming seriously hard work.

Primrose plastered on a smile. Only a few months ago she was happy with this life - just because some hippies moved in next door was no reason to think life on the other side of the grass would be any better.

George came in and asked her if she was feeling any better. The house was quiet. Annabelle was at Bible classes and Christian was doing homework. The house was orderly and quiet, just the way George liked it. Dinner was organised and outwardly life seemed perfect. Little did they know that Christian was playing *Fortnite* with his friends online, and Annabelle had decided Bible class was not for her and had met Rae and other friends from school at the local café!

George was keen for a chat while the house was quiet. He sat down at the kitchen table while Primrose continued to prepare the family meal. He could tell Primrose had something on her mind, but really could not be bothered with asking what it was for fear of a long-winded 'downer' discussion. He knew life was not meant to be easy all the time; it's just something we have to do right most of the time. A few slip-ups were forgivable, but repeating them becomes a bore. Primrose has been acting a little strange for a few weeks.

George spoke quietly. "How are you feeling about our next meeting?"

Primrose shook her head. "I am not sure I can make it."

George sounded annoyed. "Well I can't really go alone. It's not how the lessons work. We have so much to learn and we will become outsiders if we don't make a regular appearance."

"I'm sorry, I really have been feeling under the weather. I will see how I feel tomorrow. Let's just see how things are tomorrow, George."

"I want you to feel comfortable with this. We discussed how it won't work if we don't share the experience. All the couples need to journey together and experience the steps side by side to find heightened awareness."

Primrose dropped her eyes to the table. She had always been happy to share everything with George, but this 'enlightening journey' was proving to be more complicated as the weeks progressed.

Annabelle strolled through the front door. She was really not in the mood for her parents and their questions. She felt like her world was turning in the exact opposite direction to the one they wished her to follow. Rae was becoming an obsession of late, and she could see herself happy for once, not following rigid and obsessive rules. Today they had simply sat together and chatted and laughed about school and life. Laughter - something she rarely heard within the walls of her own family home.

George stared at Annabelle as she entered the kitchen. His eyes were intense and made her feel as though he could look right inside her, exposing all her untruths and sins.

He spoke with equal intensity. "Annabelle. How was Pastor Dan's class? What topic are you covering at the moment?"

It was not really in Annabelle's make-up to lie. Yet lately she was learning to do it with a lot of sincerity.

"Great, dad. Hi, Mum. We were discussing population growth in Third World countries and how the church is teaching the people to live a Christian life and providing them with clean water, helping them build houses and setting up farms for them to learn how to grow their own food."

Her parents looked pleased with the content of the discussion and left it there. Annabelle felt bad that she was lying to them, but she knew if she told the truth they would not let her see Rae, and her life would simply return to how it was. It was not something she wished to think about. Her Bible class had discussed

Third World countries and how the church was helping the week before, so it was a partial truth. Her father seemed happy enough, so she left them to get back to their own private discussion. Something was not right with her parents lately, so she was happy to not linger.

THE BROOKS

Next door, the Brooks were sitting down to a healthy meal Rae and Cee had prepared for their parents. They had made a warm pumpkin, pepita and feta salad, and baked the dough their mum had left resting before she left this morning. Warm, nut-filled bread left a beautiful aroma throughout the house. A bunch of wildflowers Cee had collected on her way home from school sat in the middle of the table in a small milk jar. As his parents sat down to eat, Rae thought his father looked very weary. His mother said he had been sick on and off following the treatment. But he still managed a huge smile and greeted Rae and his sister with a big kiss on their cheeks. He told them how beautiful the table looked, and thanked them for putting in such a huge effort to help mum. It was very much appreciated.

After acknowledging all there was to be grateful for, the family ate. It hadn't been Handel's best day, but it may not be his worst. He had made it through with the help of his family and his internal strength. He knew he could beat this disease.

Life can be a struggle, yet when family sit, discuss, cry and laugh together, each day is bearable. Without support, nothing seems possible. Handel looked around the table and felt anything was possible with these beautiful humans beside him each day.

He got up from the table and plastered a huge sloppy kiss on each of their divine faces and felt happy - despite feeling like throwing up again. He said goodnight and retired to the bedroom with a bucket beside his bed. Sunnie came and lay quietly next to him and he felt peaceful. Life was OK.

Rae and Cee cleared the table and went to the kitchen to do the dishes together. Cee whispered to Rae. "I am so scared dad is going to die."

Rae hugged her. A tear fell down his own cheek. "I am scared too. To feel like you may lose someone you have loved from the moment you were born is one of the biggest, scariest things we will ever have to face. When you want to cry, cry. When you have questions, I am always here for you. We are all feeling the same thing. Fear of what we don't know."

They set about doing the dishes in silence, each with thoughts of losing their dad, yet knowing they were all there for each other took the edge off just a little bit.

A soft scent of salt air drifted through the open window as Handel lay his head on the pillow. He closed his eyes and could see the full waves rolling towards the shore and heard the tremendous crash as the sea met the land and the sand shifted. A silence could be heard momentarily until the next set of waves. Handel visualised what he loved. The ocean he missed so much surrounded him as his mind swam in a beautiful but wild sea; his body supported and his mind at peace. Quickly he drifted off to sleep as darkness soothed his weary mind.

Sunnie watched him sleep. She was more in love with this beautiful man each and every day. He always had looked on life as an experience which helps us grow. Simply look to the sun and the moon to guide you through both the light and the darkness, as they both shine to guide us. The sun wakes us each day to possibility, while the moon shows us that even in darkness, we will find light. His words whispered in her mind as she lay by his side ready to fight alongside him and win this latest challenge in their life.

Even when the day has been hard and you know the next one may be harder still, sleep will allow you to wake to believe a new day, a new beginning, new possibilities are still reachable if we take life by the hand and gently lead it to where you want to go.

Sunnie believed this, for to not believe gave no sense of purpose to the following day. Her mind was scattered, yet she knew as long as she had this man by her side, she would love him with every bit of her heart and make this journey as easy as possible. Love conquers all and we will all end up in the same place - just at different times. With this thought her mind and her breathing slowed as she too drifted into the darkness of night.

Rae had fallen asleep with a book in his hand beside his little sister. Dreaming and restless, Cee moved her arm, hitting Rae on the brow. He stirred and tucked Cee under the covers, then quietly crept into his own room. The night was still and the moon was bright in the sky, its light falling onto his bedcovers as though it was showing him where to place his worried mind. He tried to sleep but his thoughts simply would not leave. It was like they had been waiting all day to leap from one to another. He looked through the curtain to the moon and as the light fell upon his face, he felt the peace that only something larger than life can bring. As he realised his power was tiny compared to the powers of the universe, he too finally relaxed and drifted under the light of the moon into peaceful bliss.

THE ROBINS

As the sunlight peeked through the curtains, George opened his eyes slowly to the light of day. Stark realities hit hard as he looked at his wife wrapped in the sheets, teetering on the other side of the bed. They had felt so distant from one another in the past month. Everything he had tried to do to bring them closer was slowly tearing them apart. The meetings had shown them some intimacy. Then their new neighbours had arrived like a hurricane and torn tradition apart as they had known it. What was he to do? Throughout their marriage they had lived by a week-to-week routine. Working, going to church and socialising within their comfort zone of the church community. Yet as time had crept along, cracks started appearing, and as quickly as George tried to repair them another would appear. This latest set of evil had been causing the hairline fracture of their relationship to slowly widen with each and every day. No matter how loud he yelled or how strongly he set the boundaries within the family it seemed each of them were choosing to jump outside the lines. The world he had known was being tested and those he loved were choosing to extend themselves and live outside his control. This was shifting his world and he was not liking it one bit. Something had to change.

He got up to start the day the way he liked it to start. This included a wife awake beside him and happy to start the day with him. Primrose slowly untangled herself from the sheet and sat on the side of the bed listening to the footsteps of her children and the birds chirping to greet the day. How could the sun shine, the sky be cloudless, while she felt inside her the stirrings of a storm that had come to settle in?

George was distant and brooding, his voice clipped and demanding. Primrose was doing everything in her power to keep the morning light and effortless, yet she knew one wrong move and the battle would be on.

Tempted by the smell of toast, Annabelle and Christian walked into the kitchen and took their place at the table. They could immediately see the grim face of their father staring at them both, with a face full of intent and unspoken words.

He spoke in a monotonous tone, asking what plans they had for today. Without waiting for an answer, he went straight into command mode and demanded both of them listen. There were to be no interruptions and he was not up for any negotiations at the end of the conversation. This was not to be a discussion, simply a direction to be followed completely.

"Our family is special. As your parents, we want only what is best for you both. So I am letting you know that, apart from school, any social interaction with the riffraff next door is banned. They do not share the values we want instilled into our family. This is not up for discussion - simply abide by the rule."

Christian's face fell and his eyes welled. Annabelle simply stared at her father in shock. Why would he make this blanket rule without discussing the issue? We are more than capable of choosing our own friends. It will simply make us deceitful and hide our feelings from him more. Why does he feel the need to protect us from such caring, warm, gentle people? It makes no sense and simply makes us retreat from him as a father. Does he not see he is making all of us sad, especially our mother?

Annabelle was already fighting the demons in her head regarding Christianity and how it excludes and judges. Nothing was making any sense to her, as she had always believed that we must love our neighbour and show kindness to others, yet here was her father banning these people who showed compassion, warmth and so much joy – something severely lacking in her own home life. Anyway, no point in reacting. Annabelle knew she could manoeuvre her life around the ban. It meant being deceitful and lying, which she hated to do, but it was a necessity to stay sane in this household.

This man was controlling, overbearing and angry. To her he was her father and she had always looked up to him, though now as she matured, it was getting harder to respect him. Rae was the epitome of everything she loved about life. Joy bubbled up inside him like a fountain and spilled on to everyone that stood next to him. How can this be bad? He was fun, adventurous, had a cheeky wit and a smile that transported you to where only sunshine shone. *Feels like heaven to me, and we have always been told that as good people that is where we will end up.* She was not giving that up for a father who allowed no one an opinion of their own.

Through the kitchen window, her eye caught a glimpse of Rae waltzing down the path. Her father continued to speak sternly to her. Life stopped momentarily as reality sunk in. She was becoming her own person and questioning the ways of those that she had always believed in one hundred per cent. This was what causes all the angst in our teenage years. She had always had great respect for her parents and followed their way with all her heart. Life was changing so quickly it was like a merry-go-round that had suddenly sped up and was spinning around with no way to escape or stop. She kept going around and around and getting nowhere and all she wanted to do was escape and get on another ride that would gently meander and allow her time to think. Her father's face was distorting like those in the funfair mirrors, and she could hear his voice rising to a large roar. She looked into his face and his anger was making his face red and blotchy. She couldn't respond. She simply turned and calmly walked out the front door.

George was paralysed with anger. His hearing had become muffled and his vision blurred. He knew his blood pressure was rising, yet he could not control his mood. He suddenly noticed Christian shaking and crying uncontrollably. Where was Annabelle? He felt as though he had been on fast forward and had no recollection of the past few seconds. He stood quietly and felt numb. Primrose had been in the shower and heard his voice rising. She wrapped her dressing gown around her tightly, like a shield of armour, and rushed into the kitchen. Christian was shaking and sobbing quietly while George stood frozen. His face appeared pale and his eyes distant. Primrose wrapped Christian in her arms and sat down with him on the lounge.

George walked quietly from the room and out into the back-yard. Life had been escalating to this point for a while now. As the children grew, his ability to control them was decreasing and his power over them was losing its effect. George knew he needed to talk to someone quickly or he would lose everything he loved. Turmoil was encasing their lives and nothing he said or did was helping. He got out his mobile phone. Pastor Neville answered the phone immediately. George felt calmer straight away, as the Pastor's soothing voice reassured him that there is always help a phone call away. He was not alone, and others have experienced similar experiences. He gave him the number of a psychologist he knew who dealt with men facing theses changes in their lives. George thanked him and hung up. He covered his face with both of his hands and began to sob. His head dropped heavily. He was so disappointed in himself and felt that his life was going down a path that was surrounded by the deepest jungle, swamped by never-ending darkness. Maybe now was the time to open up and get rid of not only the guilt of how he was treating his family, but also his hidden past and the shame his own father had brought on him. He had locked it in the back of his mind for too long. Obviously it was weighing him down and no matter how strictly he followed the word of God, his actions were not helping him out in the here and now. Guilt was difficult to rid oneself of, and hidden guilt was even harder to shake off. It stuck to him like mud, making him feel unclean and unworthy.

Christian's sobs slowly subsided into hiccups, and he nestled quietly in his mother's loving embrace. His little world was rocked violently when the ones he loved the most yelled and screamed about things he had no capabilities of understanding. He thought Cee was the sweetest friend he had ever had. It frightened him when he could not understand the reason behind the anger. As his fear slowly subsided and his little world became secure again, his mother released him and took him by both hands.

"All will be fine, your father is simply a little upset and tired today. You know when you get exhausted and the tears tumble, well that happens to grownups, too. He will work it out and we will help him. So let's wipe away those tears and I will take you to school."

Primrose looked through the window and saw her husband with his head in his hands. She had no desire to intrude or be a part of his pity session. He had made his bed so he could lay in it until they had all processed and recovered from his extreme anger and verbal outburst.

In the meantime, as Christian's pale face and red eyes looked up at her, her children were her first priority.

She dressed quickly, took Christian's hand and they left the house with only a forward glance. No looking back. That was to be

Primrose's words to live by. As she started the car, her mind was clear, even though her stomach was turning over.

COFFEE

At the school gate Primrose was greeted with the open smile of her new fresh-faced neighbour, who looked like she had life all sorted. Sunnie was stunning, glistening with health without a touch of make-up. Her hair cascaded in perfect waves with the sunlight catching the gold. She had a spring in her step as Cee held her hand and looked up at her adoringly. Neighbour envy ate at Primrose's insides as the nausea rose to strike again. She managed a weak smile back, but she knew her eyes held sorrow, so she was not surprised when this free-spirited woman spoke with concern.

"You look like you could do with a coffee! I am heading to the local after school drop-off, and I'd love some company if you are free."

Primrose answered gratefully. " I would love that."

Sunnie, dressed in simple clothes with no adornments, contrasted greatly against Primrose, in her modestly cut floral shift dress that covered her knees, gold cross necklace and sensible flat slip-on shoes. An unlikely match for friendship, but sometimes another perspective helps to see the light.

They found a secluded table under the jacaranda tree in the café's small outdoor space. A light wind blew, and petals fell occasionally around them as they began a discussion Primrose thought she would never share with anyone. But something fragrant was in the air, a time for new beginnings, to shed the heaviness of the past. Just like a tree shedding its leaves and baring its bones, Primrose needed to do the same. She wanted to lighten her burden, and Sunnie was just the one. She had an open mind that may be able to help her make some pretty important decisions.

"Sunnie, I know we have only been friends for a short time, but I feel you are someone I can trust with a secret I never want to go further than you. Can I burden you and know it will go no further?"

For the next hour, Sunnie sat and listened. She did not judge. Inside, she wept, but outwardly she sat respectfully.

Later, as Sunnie reflected about her chat with Primrose, she thought it best to push it to the back of her mind. She had people she loved who really needed her. Handel was her concern now. He was coping with one of life's biggest challenges - a disease that may terminate his life before he had lived out his dreams. She had not mentioned his illness to Primrose, as she was lost in a far greater personal dilemma that was causing great turmoil and disturbance in her own little nest. It seemed the protection of the church was letting Primrose down greatly, and now she was finding it difficult to confide in anyone due to judgement and criticism. She was experiencing a loss of faith in everything she had grown up to believe was right and good.

Primrose was surprised at herself, confiding in someone she had known less than a few weeks, yet somehow it felt right. Sunnie was open and had choices, and with this freedom she lived a life that was wholesome and good – the opposite of what Primrose expected when they first met. She had been guilty of judgement, and this now had her stuck in a situation where if she told the truth, she could not only defame herself, but an entire institution. *Do I become a ghost, or do I become bold and face not only my community but possibly the world?* She knew how social media could take hold of many stories and create a worldwide controversy overnight.

Yet here she was. She felt ill, but life was going to play out one way or the other. Realistically, to live a lie would allow life to go on in its usual manner. No controversy, no pain and no shame. Yet doesn't that go against all the teachings of the very church that had helped create this awkward and undesirable situation?

Somehow, she had to make a decision and live by it till the day she died. Her chest felt heavy and her stomach began to convulse. She raced inside and was violently ill. She washed her face, cleaned her teeth and lay down, quickly falling asleep to dream of a life that had turned from a dream into a nightmare.

CHAPTER

18

DEFIANCE

My life is on repeat. Primrose's words kept repeating over and over to herself. Crosses, religious paintings, images of priests, nuns, angels and devils in every colour of the rainbow were surrounded by flames, while eyes shone brightly and unseen voices laughed at her, saying over and over 'pleasure brings pain'. Rosary beads were thrown at her and rough hands pulled at her until she was gasping for air ... then suddenly she was aware of hands gently stroking her forehead.

It was Annabelle. "Mum, mum, are you OK? Wake up!"

Primrose opened her eyes, her gasping ceasing as she realised she could breathe. Her pulse was still racing, and her heart was pounding in her chest. She felt disorientated in time and place, yet slowly started to settle as she took in her daughter's face and calming voice.

"Sorry, love. I was just having a nap and was in the middle of a nightmare. Glad you woke me from that one!"

"You're very hot mum, are you sick?"

"No, I'm fine, don't worry about me."

"Well, I do worry. You don't seem yourself of late."

"No, really, I'm OK. What time is it?"

"Five o'clock."

"Oh gosh, I've slept too long. Time to get ready to go to the meeting with dad. I'll jump in the shower now."

"I'll get dinner ready, mum. You don't look too well to me."

"Thanks, love."

George walked through the front door looking pale. There were dark circles under his eyes. He was concerned how Primrose would react after this morning's altercation. He knew he must take control of his family, yet he did not want to completely destroy them - and himself - in the process. He felt his role as head of the family was being challenged, and that the way he had been taught to be a man by his father was all of a sudden wrong. He should be more understanding, and not raise his voice. Discuss, not demand. Guide. 'His way or the highway' was not a good way to live life. Yet he had been raised by a father who, when he said jump, you asked, 'how high'? *When did the role of the man become so complicated? It's a role that has switched and changed with every generation, and now I am just confused.* Maybe ruling his family with anger and domination was wrong, yet he had not been taught any other way. *Does that make me a monster?* He felt as though it did. He just didn't know what to do anymore. Was it shameful for a man to hang his head and cry? *I don't want to be like this anymore,* he decided. He knew before he could change, he needed help. *But where do I start, when the one institution I have followed all my life is part of the reason I am so confused?*

Primrose looked up from preparing dinner to look straight into her husband's eyes. She feared the dark place he had entered, and was saddened by the void that was widening between them, yet she could not muster any sympathy after all the things he had done to her and the children over the years. He was a handsome man, yet the ugliness of his nature made her see a man that was unattractive to her now. *No matter how good-looking you are, your behaviour has coloured my view. You have bruised me to the core.* Primrose could see only darkness without a single star, the looming thunderclouds heavy with the tears from her tender heart. She wondered if George could see through the darkness or if he had become totally blinded to the reality of what was happening in their lives. She imagined her tears flooding his heart and drowning him in sorrow, so that he could realise how many times he had suffocated her through his controlling behaviours. She could not see a way back from this latest outburst, but she had always been taught to forgive and forget. She was perfectly willing to forgive in certain circumstances, but to forget - that was near impossible. George had burned a path of pain too deep inside her.

Her husband lifted his eyes to meet hers and spoke quietly. "I am sorry for speaking to the children the way I did, and for causing you so much pain with my anger. I am totally devastated by my actions, and have made arrangements to discuss my torment and behaviour with Pastor Neville."

Primrose took a step back. "The same Pastor Neville that recommended we join the 'Follow Your Heart' meeting group." Primrose spoke equally quietly.

"Yes, he is our spiritual leader and his advice is important to me."

"Well, I'm not sure his directions are something we should be following so intently. I am feeling that the way he is 'helping' us and the others is not the way I wish my life to move forward."

"How can you not agree with a leader who believes in the love and support of a community? 'One love among us all' is something I cannot question. Our sole purpose is to spread the word of love and help each other to discover a deeper and more meaningful life. Pastor Neville is teaching us what is not taught beyond the privacy of closed doors. That seems to me a good path to a deeper, more meaningful relationship for us. We are also helping others, so how can you question the words of a man of God?"

Primrose held his gaze. "I know it all sounds like the meetings should help us grow and explore the natural part of our existence, but I'm not sure I like the consequences of our actions.

"In any case, it is still no excuse for you to make blanket rules for our children without consulting me and us discussing it together. I have always blindly followed your ways, and I am starting to not like the outcomes of simply listening to you and others and not making judgements for myself.

"You treat us all like we are less than you. We have no voice, we are simply told what is to be done, and you treat me the same way as the children. I am a grown adult with a fully functioning mind, and I do not like being treated as though my sole purpose in life is to serve you. That is not how our country is run, and I don't want my home to run that way. We are a democracy, and I want our home to give each one of us a view and a voice to encourage a harmonious and functioning life. I have a problem, and it's growing each and every day. You are the cause, and I am beginning to resent you for what I think should never have happened in the first place. I put myself in a submissive role in this household and this marriage, and now I have to be embarrassed by the actions I took to please you. I don't know how I am going to face my children, yet alone the outside world. I should have listened to my intuition and never let you or our church manipulate me into a situation I was never comfortable with.

"So I am telling you now I will not be going to the meeting this evening, and I would rather you not go alone, despite the group saying if one partner is not available it makes for a more intimate and personal experience for the other. I don't want you to be taken in alone and shown the intimate inside of their lives. Do you understand?"

"Who are we to question Pastor Neville?" George insisted. "He has taken time out to form this therapy group, and you have seen how it has grown and progressed over the last few years. We have formed meaningful relationships within our community, and under the guidance of a man of God, learned to love in a way that many others never get to do. How can you not see that as a special gift?"

"George, I seriously think we need to decide for ourselves if these meetings are working or not. Personally, I am finding it difficult to remove myself from the intimacy of the group. Possibly you are a little less emotionally invested."

"But I am enjoying what I am learning, and I thought it had helped us regain a closeness in our intimate interactions. Clearly that has not happened for you."

Primrose wasn't standing down.

"Frankly, I really can't see the difference from the old 'keys in the bowl' scenario, but with an audience and the Pastor's approval. I find it intimidating and embarrassing. I know at the first meeting it was explained that it was to be clinical and strictly designed to help the couples. Yet somewhere deep inside me, a voice is crying out that it is wrong. Call it intuition, call it morals, call it conservatism, it all screams out in a way that makes my insides churn. Pastor Neville goes from room to room and never gives us any privacy or feedback other than telling us if we keep procreating, the world will be a better place. I have done my bit for the world, and I would like to feel my only purpose in life is not merely to breed and pleasure my man. The fact that at Pastor Neville's discretion we are instructed who we must swap with and what we must do goes against my marriage vows. Yet we are told it is 'Love' in its purest form.

"It may be Pastor Neville's version of 'purest form', as he doesn't break *his* vows, he just watches and does not participate. As an intelligent woman, I would like to be able to refrain from making love with another man, despite the Pastor's view that it helps us understand how others make intimacy work.

"So if you do decide to go to tonight's meeting, you go solo."

George looked deep into Primrose's clear eyes and saw she was serious. It was true – all their values had been tested by these meetings and intimate encounters, and despite them delving into a deeper understanding of love and how others love, it seemed to have headed them towards the path of doom and lovelessness. Their Christian values of 'love one another' and 'love thy neighbour' had suddenly taken a twist - George was fairly sure he'd seen Primrose looking with lust at Handel. George felt vulnerable. He was the one that had opened the door, and now it seemed to be shutting in his face with force.

He cursed the disruption the Brooks had brought to his peaceful life. There always seemed to be sun shining through their windows and laughter oozing out every crack. Why, when they dressed like they did and ran around with their bare feet touching the earth, hair free and flowing and with little knowledge of city life, did they exude such confidence and warmth? They were misfits in this life, thought George, yet despite looking different to everyone else, they had a manner that allowed them to slip right into any situation and instantly allow others to warm to them.

If he was honest, George was just a little bit jealous of this warm and loving family. He would never have chosen their life, or their values, yet here he was, surrounded by unhappiness, tears and conflict, with a family in crisis. While next door at 'Sunnyville', life appeared to be bloody perfect. Some things were just too confusing.

Primrose, exhausted, was happy to see George quietly leave the house and head to his precious meeting, which only a few months ago was going to bring peace and joy to both of them.

THE MEETING

George slipped into the front door of the church and quietly made his way towards the three rooms at the back. The door to the larger communal room was open, and inside, three couples sat quietly while Pastor Neville readied himself for the evening discussion. Cleansing incense sticks burned and quiet music played in the background. Pastor Neville cleared his throat and began to speak.

"Welcome back to you all. We will start this evening's meeting with a prayer. Please close your eyes and join me in thanking the Lord for us being able to understand and explore the loving relationships of others so that we may understand more about our own; to learn what a loving relationship in a physical sense needs in order to make it lasting. Let us open our minds and our hearts to others, so that we can feel a deep sense of connection to them and allow them to help us on our individual journey.

"Tonight we will be connecting in a very private way. What happens here will go no further than these doors. These sessions may be unconventional, yet through them the practical lessons will bring to you a new understanding of intimacy that we cannot teach through texts.

"In this session, I wish for you to communicate with someone you have not been intimate with before. Allow them, through your words, to experience a pleasure brought about by giving to another in the most selfless manner. Through this communication, you will make a connection that is so deep it connects you in a way no other can.

"Talk quietly, be respectful and do not rush the other person. George, you are alone tonight so I need one couple who would be willing to perform this lesson as not two, but three. This will mean you need to be extremely open in your communication and talk things through explicitly so that no one feels pressured. Consent is one of the most important rules in these sessions. We must respect that each individual has the right to say no, even within marriage. If you feel uncomfortable, speak up."

George was not sure about any of this, but he knew in his heart it must be right. Since he was a young child, he had been taught that the church was always right. So despite a deep stirring in the pit of his stomach – which anyone else would recognise as intuition and heed it - George was willing to participate. He knew if it helped his marriage and the church was behind it, it must be good and right.

He made his way to Room Three, where he was assigned with Melissa and Doug, a lovely couple who had joined the church a few years ago and become friendly with the Robins. They were experiencing intimacy issues following the birth of Chelsea, their second child; Melissa was tired all the time and never felt good about herself after her body had changed. Doug had become moody, angry and impatient with them all. It was he who had spoken with Pastor Neville, who thought his 'couples therapy' meetings may help them.

Melissa was a quiet, dark-eyed beauty. George knew he would really have to be respectful here, as this could be an awkward situation for Doug. He was certainly not used to another man being in the room when he was intimate, and to have Pastor Neville there as well meant the evening was going to be quite unusual, to say the least.

George changed into a robe and sat down on the edge of the couch. Melissa spoke to him from the other side of the room.

"Hi, George. These meetings have helped us a lot and we are quite comfortable with each other. Having you here may help us show you how we have discovered to be more open, and how to let each other know what we need and what gives us pleasure. It has allowed us to be more connected. If you feel you could help, please let us know and we may invite you to join us, but really neither of us has any desire to have sex out of our marriage, despite Pastor Neville's assurance it is consensual and within the walls of the church."

George felt relief. He thanked Melissa and said he was happy to simply sit and learn. He and his wife were having intimacy issues, which was why they had joined the meetings in the first place. He felt he was no longer a man. Stress had caused impotency and he had difficulty pleasuring her. Tears filled Melissa's eyes. She felt his pain.

"We were both brought up in very strict homes where sex was never spoken of," she explained.

"We were virgins on our wedding day, and we were never comfortable to explore, as we felt dirty. We have never explored our own bodies, so to explore another's felt quite uncomfortable. We want to free ourselves of our restraints and inhibitions and past feelings about sex, and open ourselves up to enjoyment and the closeness that comes with enjoying a healthy sex life. Maybe our recent inability to conceive may improve, as we would love to extend our family."

Doug also tried to put George at ease.

"Melissa and I have found these meetings so helpful, despite the unorthodox way they are held. I'm happy to have you in with us, yet I find it confronting, as nudity is something I am not altogether comfortable with at the best of times. I find it difficult in front of my wife, let alone another male. So maybe we could just talk tonight. The three of us could discuss what we have discovered over the past few weeks, and how it has helped us as individuals and couples. I know you and Primrose did the 'exchange' earlier in the course. Then, if we all feel at ease, we may explore this next step. In the meantime, if Pastor Neville comes in, maybe we could just open our robes and spoon. Just to show that we are happy with flesh to flesh. Not flash to flash!"

Reassured by their frankness, George spoke up. He told them that he and Primrose were also experiencing problems. There had been a lot of disrespect, anger and disharmony recently around raising their two children. He wanted them raised as he had been, and it was leading to a gulf not only between him and Primrose, but also between him and his children. He felt they were all trying to avoid him. They never came and instigated conversation with him, they simply left him alone in the lounge room, reading alone. It was making him feel very isolated and alone, despite being surrounded by his family.

"Sounds like we need a group hug," said Melissa. So they all dropped their robes and held each other tight. There was huge relief for each of them as Pastor Neville made his appearance in the doorway. He smiled and left the room, pleased to see his unconventional therapy working in a positive manner.

Meanwhile, Primrose sat quietly at home waiting for George's return. Her resentment was growing. George had been more than happy to go the meeting alone, and it stirred feelings of jealousy in her. Maybe she did still care. Yet she was not sure he was going to be accepting of the news she had been hiding. She knew that he would be keen to attempt intimacy when he returned, and she needed to be responsive. She needed her inner secret to remain just that – a secret - or her family would be destroyed and shamed; something she was not prepared to live through.

But how long could she keep it hidden?

THE BROOKS

The Brooks family were congregated in the kitchen. Handel was now able to keep his food down, and was enjoying the outcome of Sunnie's day in the kitchen. Fruits of the season and salads brimming with colour and goodness decorated the bench as they all sat to eat and chat. Warmth filled the room, and the laughter and chatter expelled any signs of doom and gloom from residing within, even though sickness had settled into a comfy chair. They were all hoping to shift this temporary visitor out into the fresh air where it could be swept away into the expanse of the universe, believing that through positive thinking, healthy eating and a dose of western medicine they could beat this disease. Today's daily medicine was time and patience and lots and lots of love and laughter, and they were all ready to give plenty. The family lived what they preached - live for now and live and love well, with no regrets, no resentment and no negativity.

Anyone standing outside would see a picture of a happy, healthy family soaking up the joys of each other's company, laughing, listening, full of life and enjoying a generous meal with each other. It was an image that was picture-perfect – yet, as with every family, they had their own battles to fight.

Sunnie's mind slipped away into the life of another. What Primrose had told her had shaken her. She and Handel loved making love in every way; it was an integral part of their relationship. Without that love, her children and family would have never been created. Her heart had been opened to a huge love that was itself created by love. No one can really explain the depth of a mother's love, but maybe - just maybe - if it does not come from love, the love starves and joy and happiness may never be experienced.

Primrose had been placed in a situation that had complicated her life and broken her heart. She had told Sunnie that she and George had lost what they started with; through turning to the church, their foundation had been rocked by the very thing that was meant to keep them grounded and happy. Their simple God-loving family had now been put into a position of embarrassment, not only for themselves, but for their community.

Love freely, love wholly and love without conditions. Be open to all possibilities and never feel ashamed of wanting to love someone with your whole heart. That is what Sunnie's own mother had taught her. Be kind and respectful and practice safe sex. Always carry a condom. She laughed inwardly at the memories of her wise words.

Where had George and Primrose's church been living the past century? Love should not be something hidden and deceitful and shameful. But that was what they were making it, despite acting to help these people. These meetings were supposed to help couples explore themselves and others, yet they had not taught them about the emotional complications or contraception. They had led them down the path of 'free love' and now one of their most conservative followers was facing a personal crisis.

Sunnie had always found country life and country people to be accepting of anyone, happy to include anyone with a good heart and a generous spirit. Nature provided its own lessons in love, childbirth and nurturing. But here in the city, big cracks were appearing everywhere and Sunnie was shocked by how sheltered Primrose's life had been, despite living among so many people and diverse cultures. She was realising those reared in the big city stuck to their own crowd and were not very accepting of newcomers. Primrose had kept her life private to the point of having no one close enough to tell her deepest darkest secrets, which is why her new neighbour of only a few weeks had been drawn into a secret web of lust, lies and deception.

OMG, thought Sunnie. I thought I had heard and seen most things, yet this delved into an area of perversion that was shocking even to her. Even though she had liberal views on most things in life, she did not quite know where to start in advising her new friend. She had simply listened today and suggested they get together tomorrow for lunch.

"Mum, are you with us?" Rae could see his mum had drifted into one of her frequent daydreams.

"Yes, all good. Sorry, I think I need an early night guys. Come on Cee, time for a story and bed."

AN APOLOGY

George arrived home to darkness and stillness. No one watching TV or sitting up doing homework. He quietly removed his shoes and walked into the bedroom, where Primrose lay still with a book hiding her face. She did not go to put the book down or try to engage in conversation. *She's waiting for an apology,* thought George. He leaned over to place an arm over her Primrose's body. She always liked to be shown affection with a hug, and he could then gauge whether he was being invited to go to the next stage. She did not draw away or fend him off with her arm, so he drew her closer and began kissing her. She responded, reluctantly at first. But slowly their bodies melded together in familiarity, and they began the rhythm of life; their bodies responding in unison. The song of climax echoed softly off the walls, and as they melted into one, George felt connected again.

"I'm sorry," George whispered. "Life has become too complicated lately, and I really would like it to just slip back to where we were when we first met. Somehow we left it behind and have become trapped by the mundane and everyday routine of work and kids."

Primrose responded. "Yes, we need to keep our intimacy open and our communication free from restraint. Let's sleep on it and start fresh tomorrow." But she felt yet again she was playing the role of the submissive wife, saying what George expected her to. The old resentment flickered, and she felt emptier than ever.

They both whispered their blessings and George, at least, slipped into a relaxed, quiet slumber.

SECRET LOVE

The morning sun crept into Annabelle's room, inviting her to play. Rae had texted her, asking her to join him at the beach for a morning meditation and swim. Without hesitation, she responded with anticipation and delight and slipped quietly from the house. It was a fair ride to the beach, and despite the early start, the sun was creeping higher into the sky with each progressing moment. The warmth beaded perspiration upon their brows as they rode in the morning rays of a day they both intended to enjoy together. Secret love was not Annabelle's intention, but with the way her parents were behaving at the moment she needed this more than anything. Carefree chatter, warmth, smiles, laughter - that's what she wanted her life to be about, not restrictive rules that made her feel as though she was being put in chains to serve her parents and a God she was having difficulty believing in at the moment.

The ride refreshed her senses, and Rae was just that added breath of fresh air she needed to fill her up. The last hill had been climbed, and now the descent to the cool shore. The waves were crashing out over the reef, and people were already strolling along the shore and bathing in the shimmering water. Annabelle and Rae looked at each other, and laughed as they let their bikes take them down the steep descent, with the wind blowing on their faces and their arms outreached either side. Their shouts of happiness filled the air as they let go of all restrictions and enjoyed the freedom of youth. These were the moments of total disregard for the restrictions of life; the moments that made everything worthwhile - a feeling that totally absorbed you and soaked you in the joy of life.

The bottom of the hill eased them to a normal pace and they both kicked in their pedal power to reach the scrub at the edge of the dunes. Quickly they lay down their bikes and, taking each other's hand, ran and dumped their towels on the sand before diving into the cool, refreshing waves. The water slipped over their bodies as they surfaced and looked at each other with huge grins. Rae grabbed Annabelle around the waist, brought her close to him and kissed her gently on the side of the cheek.

"I just want you to know that even though you have only been in my life a few weeks, you are bringing so much sunshine that my days feel endless. I want to fill my every moment with you in them. You are the daisy I would pick every time!"

Annabelle simply smiled at him. What could you say to that? He spoke from his heart, making her feel as though there was nobody else around. *This has got to be what they call love,* she thought.

Annabelle my sweet girl
Play with me in the sea
Where my heart sings love songs
And my mind roams free.

Rae's voice carried on the wind with a lilt that carried Annabelle's heart to places it had never been before. She had no thoughts of home, her parents or that she was somewhere she should not be. Everything in this precise moment was exactly as it should be. They ran up the sand dripping with the waters of youth and the salt of the earth within them. Anyone with age on their side watching them would admire their ability, beauty and freshness, and their total disregard for the rest of the world.

They lay side by side, chatting about music, friends and all the things that mattered to them at seventeen. Today was about forgetting about their parents and the problems each of them were facing, and soaking up the emotions of young love. It's something we only experience for a few years, and it's big. So many firsts and huge emotions that go along with it, be it that first kiss or the first tiff. For now, it was sweeping Annabelle out into waters she had never swum before and she felt cool, refreshed and calm. No logic, simply emotions that swept her up and wrapped her in the softest cocoon that made her feel so secure. She just wanted to lay there with the sun touching her all over. Rae was a good one for bringing out the warmth in everything.

Life away from the worrying turmoil of home was great. Yet it still concerned her that her mum had been feeling so unwell of late and that her dad was being so moody and angry. He had always been controlling, yet something else was brewing and it was deep. She could tell Rae, but being here with him made her feel like she had left the rest of the world behind, like she could move freely forward with few cares.

Like Annabelle, Rae was thinking about his own dad. Handel was good at putting on a brave front, and their family had always seen the best in every difficult situation, but when your dad's mortality was being tested, it all became very worrying. Yet here he was with a beautiful girl who he was becoming very close to, very quickly. He felt he could share his burdens with her and they would be safely locked away from the rest of the world. She would hold them in her heart and only he would have the power to open it. So he felt that all the secrets he shared with Annabelle would be safe, and, as they say, a trouble shared is a trouble halved. So maybe he could let her know about his dad's treatment. Maybe it would help ease his troubles. He loved his father more than the air he breathed, and it was making him gasp for air to think he may not share his life for much longer.

He looked into Annabelle's eyes, seeing the sincerity and trust there. He opened his mouth to speak. A small tear escaped his eyes and she noticed straight away.

"What is the matter?" She leaned forward to place a gentle hand upon his shoulder.

He hesitated for just a moment, but realised that if he did not take this opportunity his secret would eat him away.

"I am going to share something with you that you cannot tell another living soul."

Annabelle nodded, her eyes full of concern.

"My Dad has been diagnosed with cancer. He has started treatment and we're hoping his outcome will be great, but at this stage everything that lies ahead of us is unknown. I am finding it difficult to deal with, along with being at a new school and making new friends and adjusting to living in a big new city. I am feeling a little overwhelmed, and wanted to share this with you. Smiling at the world each day is becoming just a little bit difficult. Yet when I am with you it's different. My family is awesome, they make the difficulties seem easy and we always know that whatever doesn't kill you makes you stronger. Yet change is hard for us all. I know my family wanted to keep this secret, yet you are someone I feel I would like to share everything with, even my troubles."

Annabelle listened, processed, and thought how she should best respond.

"I am so sorry. Your dad looks like the picture of health, and always seems so happy. As a family you are all just so wholesome and down to earth. You come from the country, where you've lived a life full of activity. Your dad is the last person I would think this would happen to."

Rae spoke quietly, explaining that cancer does not always discriminate. It strikes quick and fast and people who you would least expect are given devastating news. Some will respond well to the treatment, while others do not.

"Cee and I have only just found out. My parents have been waiting for all the test results and treatment before they told us. So that is the reason we moved to the city. The small hospital in Dangarup didn't have access to the treatments and machines for diagnosing Dad's condition. I did think it strange we were leaving the coast and our farm but I just thought mum and dad wanted us to experience a different lifestyle; they like us to experience the world for ourselves, rather than just trusting others' opinions on things. They say if you don't give everything a go, you are depriving yourself of something that may be your true passion. Mum and dad's passion for the surf meant the ocean was never far away. Dangarup gave us rolling hills that fell straight into the sea, and fresh country air. Our life was fed by the natural earth, and we have always believed it to be the natural way to stay healthy. Now we've moved to the city, we are having to believe in western medicine, when we have always used what nature has provided. Our whole belief system is being questioned and that shift is huge."

Annabelle put her arm loosely around Rae's shoulder. "Life is so unfair sometimes. It just seems so wrong that someone like your dad, who is so easy-going, carefree and loving has to go through this. I love your family and how loving and open you all are. Mine is such a closed book and we live by so many rules created by a church and a God whose existence I question at times. You love openly and experience life by living it, and by making your own mistakes and learning from them. I have to follow the rules and never put myself in a situation that causes me, or others, any anguish. Sometimes I feel suffocated. Your family to me seems to have everything sorted, yet you still have situations that are soul destroying. If you need to talk, I am always here for you."

"Thanks Anna. Nobody's life is perfect; what's important is how we deal with each problem that we face. I am happy dad has listened to the doctors and is combining modern medicine with his own natural therapies. Love and family are also a huge healer. Sometimes my parents only follow what the earth provides. If it does not begin its life within the roots of the earth, they feel it does not belong in our bodies. What the earth provides is all we need. It's not a bad philosophy, but thanks to science we can now assist nature, and my parents are now more open to what the great minds have discovered. So hopefully my dad will live a longer life.

"So despite our amazing life, full of clean ocean air and living off the earth, Dad is still sick. Sometimes life just dishes out challenges, but they can make us stronger.

"As to your family, they are doing what they believe is right for you. All parents do things differently, no way is absolutely right, as long as they love you and do you no harm, it can't all be bad. I am still finding the God thing a little too abstract, yet I get that they believe in kindness, caring and respect - and that is good. Right? Time to get on our bikes. Everyone comes into our lives for a reason, so let's just enjoy the moments we have together. It may not be forever but it's for the here and now. So let's ride like the wind, let the breeze blow on our faces, and kiss the day smack bang on the lips!"

Annabelle knew that she would have been missed at home by now, but really could not care less. She was sick of having life spoiled by her parents and their pessimistic attitude to a life we only get one chance at living. *So here's to living and enjoying what I have right here right now!*

MOMENT OF TRUTH

Riding back down the steep hill towards home, Annabelle felt the wind clear her mind. There had been too much thinking - more doing and enjoying was on her agenda now!

But on arriving home, she felt her stomach turn and tighten. Things seemed quiet and peaceful, yet she knew once she went inside, things would change. She parked her bike in the garage and quietly entered the house by the rear door. There was not a sound in the house. Where was everyone?

As she walked lightly past her parent's bedroom door, she saw her mum sleeping peacefully on the bed. Her dad was in the lounge, reading quietly in his recliner in his nook by the window. He did not look up or say a word as he heard her pass.

Woah, this is a bit unusual. She had been gone all day, yet they were both in their own worlds and not concerned about her at all. Something big is going down if this was the only reaction to her going off all day. Even her little brother was quiet in his room.

She heard her mother stir and step into the bathroom, closing the door behind her. There was the sound of violent retching. Should she ignore it, or go in and offer some help? She knew she should at least call out, yet her parents had hardly been friendly of late.

She decided to whisper through the door. "Mum - are you OK? Do you need some help?"

Primrose was startled to hear her daughter's voice. "I'm fine love. Just must have eaten something that has not agreed with me, that's all."

She hung her head sadly over the toilet bowl. This is so wrong, she thought. I have no idea how I am going to get myself out of this situation. So many people are going to be hurt by my actions. Shame overtook her and she began to tremble violently before the next wave of nausea took hold. Misery enveloped her as her head spun and her mind went into total panic. Who was she to tell her daughter who she could befriend, when she had allowed herself to get into this situation?

Slowly the nausea passed and she got up, walked into the bathroom, undressed, and stood under the shower, allowing the hot water to wash over her body, calming and cleansing her before she did what she knew she must.

After her shower, Primrose entered the lounge, dressed in her nightwear. She drew the other recliner over close to her husband and asked if she could interrupt his reading for a while. George looked into her face, glad that she wanted to talk. She normally left him alone in the corner, and sometimes he had wished so hard for her to interrupt him and show him some attention. Primrose looked a little pale to him, and she appeared nervous. She spoke quietly, but with urgency.

"George, I need to tell you something. I don't want you to get angry or react, I simply want you to sit and hear me out and then I promise you can talk.

"We have been through some rough times of late. For some time, our intimacy has been lacking and our communication poor. We started out in life young and vital and our goals were similar. Now I simply feel we are co-existing, searching for something we once had and want back. Each new day takes us somewhere where we both feel comfortable, but not necessarily where we want to be.

"I have wanted to please you, and in doing so I have followed you down a path I never felt comfortable with. Now the consequences of that have given us both a new problem. I have thought about this long and hard, and was in a dilemma as to how – or even if - I should discuss it with you.

"Our life has centred around living and raising our family within the constraints and rules of our church. I am now going to be judged and shamed by that same church that has hidden its own shameful practices. The church is so much bigger than us, it's our whole community, and we are accepted because of the way we live. Yet now we have entered something not spoken about or even known about by the community. We could damage the church and its standing. We may be ridiculed and called hypocrites if everyone turns against us due to the shame."

George took her hand gently and clasped it in his.

"Primrose, we are together forever, and whatever you are afraid of we will face it together. If it means our family stays together, I will try and change. Maybe I have been too rigid and wanted more than should be expected of a family in today's world. It's fast, it is changing and I need to make sure our children fit in and feel they have the freedom to be who they wish to be - within reason of course."

Primrose's mouth went to open, but she could not speak. She felt the salt in her mouth and realised the dam had broken. There was no going back from here. The shame and guilt was only going to grow. Or should she take her secret to the grave, and learn to accept what is done is done, and no one but herself need know the truth? So many people live with lies and still live a good life, covering up the guilt. Truth or lies? She had lived her whole life believing in 'the truth, the whole truth and nothing but the truth'.

Yet in this moment, her choice would compromise the very security and future of her family.

THE BROOKS

Rae woke and his heart felt good. It was beating strong and he felt happy from the tip of his toes right up to the warm and fuzzy thoughts dancing in his head. He heard laughing and chattering in the kitchen, so he swung his legs out of bed and followed the scent of warm bread.

"Morning my gorgeous son." Sunnie greeted him with her usual ruffle of his hair and a peck on the cheek. Cee grabbed him around the waist, and his dad gave him a warm hug. Wow, this was going to be a good day.

"There is sun shining in your eyes today - something has warmed your heart and is letting the world know about it." Rae's mother smiled, warmth and sincerity in her voice.

"Wouldn't have anything to do with a pretty young lady next door, would it?" his father teased.

Rae smiled and laughed. "Where is my morning bread? No talk till I have something to fire up this empty stomach!"

Handel buttered a large slice of freshly toasted bread and smeared it with Vegemite, just the way Rae liked it. Not too thick - but not too thin either.

"So?"

Rae grinned and dropped his eyes to the floor. Coy and shy was something he had never been in his life.

"Well?" asked Cee. "Where were you all day with Annabelle? I missed you."

"We went to the beach, little sis, and we rode so it was a bit difficult to bring you along. Next time for sure."

Handel listened to the chat. He was feeling good today. The treatment was helping for now, so they were all happy about that. Each day they woke up to each other's warmth and humour, and this morning was no different. Handel's fine form meant Rae was his target.

"OK son, this school we have sent you to is really getting to you. 'Love thy neighbour' is obviously one of the commandments you have decided to take to heart."

They all laughed and so did Rae. What could he reply to that?

Cee was bouncing around the room, doing some new dance routine and singing. Sunnie sat quietly, contemplating her discussion with Primrose. The implications on her life if she spoke the truth could ruin her marriage, her family and also the community they felt so comfortable within. Yet why would you allow a large institution to get away with such a despicable act, even if the intention behind it was to help people? There are trained professionals that can help marriages and the problems they endure. Why would a church minister think he could do a better job? This was a problem that could become a never-ending avalanche if the truth was to be revealed. Sunnie realised she'd definitely need another coffee date - and a long one - to help Primrose solve this one.

She smiled at Handel, who seemed full of his old energy. The doctors were happy with his progress. Everything was proving to follow the optimism that the doctors had promised.

These days, the 'C' word was not a death sentence for everyone. With new treatments, cancer cells can be targeted with much more accuracy. So the pendulum of hope had swung their way, and they could all look forward to spending family time in abundance. Still, there was a long road to travel, and a bit more city life to live.

Sunnie felt a diversion from her own problems might help. Her neighbours needed help. Investing time and energy in supporting others may be just what is needed at this precise moment in time. The Robins were a nice family, if not a tad conservative and rigid in their thinking. But they weren't alone - many people became entrenched within their belief system and didn't take the time to understand there are many paths that can be taken in life. Ultimately, we may all take different journeys, but we all end up in the same place. We never know what lies behind a door until we walk through it. *Not sure I want to open the door to Primrose and her fellow parishioners if this is where you end up,* thought Sunnie. But I'm sure I will learn something along the way by just being a good neighbour and listening.

She looked around the kitchen at all the smiling faces and realised they were her rainbow, all painted with different strokes and different colours, yet all full of love. Storms brewed and rain poured, but each was at their most colourful when clear skies returned once more. How lucky was she!

Slowly the four of them left the warmth of the kitchen. Rae and Cee left for school. Handel walked with them for a while before heading off to absorb the world of nature. He needed some quiet contemplation time talking to the trees and listening to the songs of nature. He missed the countryside, so the local park that wove its way among the homes and down to the sea was his haven.

CONFRONTATION

Sunnie rapped at her neighbour's front door. It was mid-morning, and she knew the children would be at school, and George would be at work.

Primrose made her way to the front door. She could see Sunnie peering through the glass.

"Just me," called Sunnie. The door opened. Primrose looked a little dishevelled. Her eyes were watery. She was clearly upset but she managed a small smile and asked Sunnie to come in.

Inside, everything was in place and looked perfect, yet something felt off. There was no evidence of anything wrong; not a book or a cushion was out of place. Yet Sunnie herself felt out of place, as though she was unwelcome, despite Primrose asking her in.

"Are you up for a walk and a coffee?" asked Sunnie. "A bit of fresh air is always good for the soul."

"Yes - I'll just get my shoes and I'll be ready," replied Primrose.

Phew, thought Sunnie. She could not have sat in this house a moment longer. It may look like a home, but it felt lacking in heart.

The pair walked side by side in silence for a few minutes, and then Primrose started to open up about her evening with George.

The floodgates were coming down, yet Sunnie still felt Primrose was holding back some crucial aspects of her dilemma. Something was hiding behind those sad eyes, and she wondered if Primrose would ever allow herself to open up to purify herself completely.

Primrose was battling. Her emotional walls were high, and she knew that to keep living her life according to the church's rules, certain things must never be disclosed. Yet if she was to live the free, pure life she wanted, she must cleanse herself completely of guilt.

She spoke softly.

"Sunnie, I am riddled with guilt and I don't know where to turn. The church is the instigator, my husband the perpetrator, and I feel like I am the traitor to my beliefs. The Pastor I listen to each Sunday as he preaches about life and all the lessons we must learn has let me down by deceiving me. The one act that brings two people together in the most loving and closest form has now placed George and I miles apart.

"Every day, I search for your freedom, your openness, and the instant joy I feel when I am with you and your tightknit, free-wheeling little family. I thought God would give me those things, yet watching you I realise joy is not a God-given right but something each of us must give to the other. I have known you for such a short time, yet I see so clearly what I have missed out on all these years by closing my eyes to the rest of the world and only accepting those who followed our way into my life. Only now can I see how I have let myself, and my family, down."

Sunnie thought hard before responding.

"Don't ever think for a moment that our family is perfect, Primrose. We love openly, laugh openly, and love each other, but like everyone else we have our problems. The one big difference is that we choose our attitude daily, and gratitude is our attitude. We are grateful for each day we wake to the birds that start their day with a song. We believe that we all have a responsibility to ourselves and to each other to give back to the earth that sustains us. What surrounds us makes us.

"I think most people simply want to be happy. We just have to understand that for a family to be happy it takes a little more effort, as individually we want and love different things. So there is a bit more give and take required. It's a balancing act - we all need more loving at some points in our lives, yet sometimes when we need that loving we are at our lowest and not the easiest to love. But family are the ones who learn to understand. It's called empathy, and we all need a huge dose at times, and heaps of patience too. Laughter is also important. I love a good smile, a huge hug and a sense of humour. Life is short, so make each moment in each day move you forward the way you wish to go. Tell each other how you feel; we all need to feel loved. It's simple really, yet we humans love to complicate things."

Sunnie suddenly stopped, reached for Primrose's hand, and gave her a huge hug, pulling her close to her heart right there in the middle of the footpath. Primrose felt so fragile in that moment. Her heart felt as if it broke in a million pieces. Tears streamed down her face, yet she felt released. She realised that for every problem, there is a solution.

As Sunnie and Primrose continued their stroll along the tree-lined street, they heard the slow approach of a car behind them. A voice called out. It was George. As he drove alongside the women, he stopped and stared at them. His eyes looked wild, glassy and he appeared on edge. His voice was high pitched, his words quick and agitated. Sunnie looked at Primrose with a puzzled look. She knew something was not quite right, and her intuition was on high alert. George pulled over, leapt from the driver's seat and grabbed roughly at Primrose. Sunnie's heart was racing and she felt extremely threatened. This was the face of anger, control, frustration; a man that had no idea of how to deal with a world he was quickly being excluded from. In this precise moment, Sunnie knew her actions would either help her friend or place her in extreme danger. Fortunately, her years of martial arts and yoga allowed her to act with an element of calm while averting the danger of an aggressive mind and body that was threatening someone weaker and more vulnerable. Her movements were precise - and extremely painful. George let go of Primrose long enough for Sunnie to grab Primrose's wrist and encourage her to run as fast as she could away from this man who was clearly not only a danger to others, but to himself.

Once out of sight, Sunnie dialled 000, gave the exact position of George and his car, and waited with Primrose.

George lay in pain, crumpled by a world that he had tried to fix. Life had become too much: too much love combined with too much confusion, too much jealousy, too much he could not control. He had lost himself in his religion and the pressures of modern society.

He was broken, and he wanted others to be broken, too.

Sirens sounded, stopping abruptly where George lay still. He was stupefied; his face was glazed and he was not responding to any verbal commands. The paramedics arrived behind the police, who had handcuffed him so he could be sedated for the trip to hospital. His aggression had subsided; now all that was left was a shell of a man, whimpering and in shock. He allowed himself to be put into the back of the ambulance with no acknowledgement of his wife or the event that had just taken place.

One of the paramedics came over to Primrose and Sunnie and asked if they knew the gentleman. Primrose was in shock and began to cry.

"He is my husband, but right now he is a stranger to me."

The paramedic turned to Sunnie.

"He will be admitted for a mental health assessment. You can bring your friend to the hospital once she is feeling up to it."

Life had certainly taken a twist for the worst.

Primrose began to feel dizzy and nauseous. She needed to sit down now or she'd fall heavily. Sunnie saw the colour drain from her friend's face and gently guided her to the bench close by. She dialled Handel - he should be home from his doctor's appointment by now.

"Hi, Handel it's me - would you be able to pick me up from Randell Park? I've been for a walk with Primrose and she is not feeling well."

"OK love, on my way now."

A few minutes later, the brightly coloured van pulled up beside them. Handel's huge smile greeted them as he ran around to open the door to let them in. He could see straight away that Primrose looked pale and distressed. Sunnie's usual bright demeanour was unusually dampened too. *There is a story here that I am sure I will hear when we get home, he thought.* Until then, silence would suffice.

As the van pulled into the Brooks' driveway, Sunnie asked Primrose to come in and have a cup of camomile tea. Primrose was more than happy for the company and comfort, so she took Sunnie's arm and they went inside. Her pulse was racing and her head was banging. She just wanted to close her eyes, and her mind – well, it was overflowing with confusing, muddled and disturbed thoughts.

Sunnie grabbed a rug and a pillow and told Primrose to lie down while she put the kettle on. Compliant, Primrose lay down and closed her eyes to the world. This was a nightmare; in her ordered, Christian life these things were foreign and frightening. She felt wretched. The morning's event was taking its toll, not only on her, but the new life that was beginning to stir inside her. Could she trust her neighbours with her secret? Dealing with a husband that was clearly not coping, and bearing a baby that was not his, was pushing her closer to the cliff every day. Her intent on this morning's walk was to unburden and ask for advice from someone totally open and impartial in their thinking. Sunnie had arrived in her life just at the right moment. As they say, people come into our lives for a reason: some may stay for the long haul and others just in passing, but they all arrive for a reason. Maybe Sunnie and Handel could put this catastrophe into perspective.

As she put the kettle on, Sunnie explained events quietly to Handel. She had known something revealing was going to be said this morning. Yet the opportunity was missed, due to George arriving and reaching breaking point. *These two people whose lives were filled with order and Christianity and values had suddenly become so vulnerable to life and its ups and downs,* thought Sunnie. Somewhere they had lost themselves, and now they were in crisis mode. Her being here and able to support Primrose meant a great deal to Sunnie. The universe had touched her and given her the gift of helping someone. How she responded could help a family rebuild their trust and happiness. Not today, but gradually, over time, if she used her love and warmth and common sense. No super magic, just abilities we all have but sometimes forget. Love and compassion for other human beings that cross our path for a reason. Sunnie possessed deep intuition, and this lady, her neighbour who was normally so collected, was not OK. *So I'll just have to ask what's up, and see if I can help.*

Making tea later in the afternoon, Sunnie looked out the kitchen window and saw four gorgeous, happy kids walking down the street. Rae, Cee, Annabelle and Christian. Christian and Cee were holding hands and skipping and laughing. Not a care in the world. Rae and Annabelle strolled behind in a world of bliss, watching over their younger siblings. They were almost home. Some hard realities were about to take hold. Primrose had slept on and off all day on the couch. Waking occasionally in tears, but not ready to talk. The shock of seeing George in that state of mind weighed heavily on Sunnie. Should she add more fuel to a fire already burning out of control?

Just outside, she could see young love blossoming and the innocence of childhood friendships and laughter frolicking out in the pure air and sunshine. At the same time, a dark storm had clouded her sunshine and it was going to take some fresh ideas to blow it out the window. It may not even be possible for Sunnie to ever rid herself of these dark clouds; they seemed to be infiltrating every fibre of her being and were completely foreign to her nature.

She thought about the journeys they were all on. While one world was collapsing, others were enjoying every moment of their being. So many journeys; each one crossing paths with others in unexpected ways and bringing joy, sadness, disappointment, contentment, acceptance, shame, fear, excitement, shock. Yet when journeys combine, pathways change, and with someone beside us, everything becomes a little easier. Some people find when they are alone that they need something more, and reach out to what many call God. This 'God' comes in different colours, different forms and with different rules, yet he serves the one purpose. To teach people to respect and to love. *My god does not have a name,* thought Sunnie. *To me, it is simply gratitude and love for the ones I am lucky to call my family. I thank the universe for its many gifts and hope I can pass this on and teach my loved ones to believe in the universe too. Many challenges will be thrown at us, and today I am facing a huge one. But with courage and support I will face whatever I have to, and help others overcome the troubles they find themselves in. Just breathe, let the situation evolve around you and don't let your light go out due to the darkness of others. Remember, this is Primrose's fight. I simply need to listen and not react. If things starts to consume me, I will simply remove myself for a while.*

As Sunnie's thoughts aligned themselves in an orderly fashion, her mood lifted once more. Her youth had helped her learn to create light whenever she needed it; not because life had been easy but because she had found herself at a young age in the middle of adult problems. Through the darkness she developed her own way of making her life full of light and colour. By staying united and strong, her family realised that with a sunny disposition on life, even the darkest days are not so bad.

AUTUMN

An early morning stillness met Primrose as she looked out of the kitchen window. Nothing moved; it was like a painting. Early autumn leaves carpeted the lawn and the liquidambar was aglow with orange, gold and yellow leaves. So much change occurring, yet the stillness gave the world a sense of peace. *These are the moments we must savour, this is when our minds can think quietly and allow the changes we make in our lives to really make a difference.*

Primrose was trying to feel strong and see a solution, yet the nausea and overwhelming tiredness was making it all that more difficult. Her natural instinct was to gather her loved ones and run as far away as possible from the source of all her unhappiness. Yet her intelligence and practical side reminded her that running only weakens your strength; it does not make you face your challenges and resolve them.

Meanwhile, each day a new life was growing from within while on the outside, life was eating her alive. How can a church that preaches goodness hide such evil while professing they are helping? George was a good man, yet he was full of pain and was so vulnerable that his vision had been clouded by a man hiding behind the institution. The whole of her Christian life she had been taught that the church and its belief system was bigger than anything on earth; it provided support when you needed it and a support group to lean on when times were tough. It provided friendships that were vital to living a valuable life. Yet now it felt like an infested river. Slowly and unseen, a poison was filtering into the waterways and the innocent were ingesting tiny amounts of filth that were gradually affecting their health and wellbeing.

I need to breathe, thought Primrose. I need to feel cool clean air, filtered by pure health and happiness, enter my spirit through nature and forget about all I have been indoctrinated with. I need to listen to my intuition. This was the hardest lesson she had ever had to learn, and it was leading her away from her belief system to an unknown and frightening place that still felt, somehow, safer than where she was.

At this moment, Primrose's intuition was telling her she had been sent an angel in the form of her new neighbour. *Sunnie has the wisdom I need to get through this difficult and sinful situation,* she thought. *No other thoughts are leading me to a peaceful end in this traumatic situation, so just listen and lean on those that are there for you right now.*

A movement in the house broke the silence. Annabelle padded out from her bedroom, wrapped up tight in her chenille dressing gown, hair tousled and cheeks flushed with the glow of youth.

"Morning, mum." Annabelle looked deep into her mother's eyes and felt a sadness dwelling beneath the surface. She quietly pulled up a stool next to her at the island bench. She didn't speak, she simply sat enjoying the solitude and peace of a house that had suffered too much torment of late. No words could take away the pain or remove the scars of yesterday, but this was a new day, a new chance to remove themselves from the evil of the past.

Annabelle knew she was oblivious to many of the real causes of her parents' situation, yet she felt it was complicated. She understood that whatever had happened was not something that was intended to hurt her and Christian. It was deep and secretive, and something that was best left alone. Her intuition led her to believe that adult problems were mysterious and beyond the teenage realm. But her compassion told her that her mum needed her more than ever. She got up from her stool and went around to where her mother sat crumpled and silent and embraced her and snuggled her head into her neck.

She whispered with her warm breath into her mum's ear. "Mum, I will always be here for you. I love you."

Primrose smiled gently. "Thank you, Annabelle. I know we have been strict on you. I am questioning things at the moment. I am prepared to change and make our lives a little less rigid. Our new neighbours have shown me that a little free thinking and freedom may help us live a happier life than the one we have been led to believe is the only way. I love you too. I will need you to be patient with me for a little longer while I sort these problems out. Your dad is not in a good place at the moment and hopefully he will now get the help he needs. Yesterday he reached a crisis and took it out on me. He has been placed in a mental health facility, and until his anger and mood swings are sorted out, he will remain there. Hopefully with time we can re-solve all our issues and life will settle back to some form of nor-mality – but a different normal to what we have forced upon you and Christian up until this point in your lives.

"I am so, so sorry." Primrose wept openly into her daughter's arms, feeling a new-found freedom as her emotions let go after years of restraint.

****

Hindsight is a great learning curve, as are mistakes. Primrose knew that the effort required to rebuild her life was enormous, but sometimes when the mistakes we make are huge, the effort to make things right need to be just as big, if not bigger. Today, she would sacrifice her pride and her secrets to try and turn her life, and her family's lives, around. But would she reveal her secrets to all? She still was not sure. 'The whole truth and nothing but the truth' may not free her completely. This secret would have lasting effects, not just on herself, but on others who were totally innocent of any injustice - the very people she wanted to protect.

The normal morning routine slowly continued. Christian and Annabelle went off to school, despite the traumatic events of the day before. Primrose had protected them as much as she could, yet they had to know that their father would not be returning home until his mental health issues improved - possibly for a few months.

Primrose hoped that disclosing her secret would allow her freedom from the trauma. But was she being selfish in drawing another family into her chaos? She wouldn't know that until she had the courage to ask for help. Something inside her whispered to her that Sunnie and Handel had entered her life for a reason. They were her guardian angels. Not that she believed in higher entities much anymore - after the way she had been treated by those in the church - yet she knew she must not lose faith in humankind. Good still existed. We just had to seek out the right people to surround ourselves with, and not be too quick to think that those who place themselves in positions of good *are* good – and at the same time, not assume everyone is bad. Life is complicated and messy, no matter what we do.

Too much thinking and not enough action, thought Primrose. So she showered, dressed and walked next door. She tapped on the front door and waited, but there was no response.

The windows were open, and Primrose could hear music quietly playing. A beautiful scent infused the air. Yet no one stirred. She decided to check around the back. As she turned the corner of the house, she saw Handel and Sunnie sitting cross-legged under the trees on a colourful Mexican-style rug. Their eyes were closed to the outside world. She could hear them humming. Primrose softly made her way towards them, without disturbing their peace. They were chanting: *Breathe in light. Breathe out darkness.*

Primrose quietly sat down near them. There was something sacred and peaceful about this, and she wanted to absorb the moment. She felt something lighten in her spirit. Everything was going to be fine. Somehow, these people were here to set things right in a world that had become far too complicated. She sat in silence for a few more minutes until Handel opened his eyes and inhaled deeply. He smiled. There it was again - that glorious smile that sent happiness into the most hardened of souls. Once she would have called these people weird hippies, yet she now knew they were a caring family with integrity and intelligence and a real desire to live in harmony with a world that was moving at a pace that was hard to keep up with anymore. They realised we didn't need to keep up – not if we just stopped and were conscious of what we needed, instead of what we desired, and were more mindful of all that surrounds us - not just the people, but also our planet.

Handel got up and embraced Primrose. Not a word spoken, yet so much passed between them - care, sorrow, understanding and compassion.

Sunnie then opened her eyes to the world and the chatter began.

"Good morning, Primrose. How are you? We try to start each day with meditation, and today it was too glorious to remain inside."

"Sorry to interrupt. I need to talk to you both about something you may find a little shocking. I am hoping, with your positive outlook on life, that maybe you can help me solve a huge problem. I was meaning to discuss it with Sunnie the other day before George was admitted to hospital. Would you have some time today?"

"I'm really sorry, Primrose, but we have an appointment in fifteen minutes. We'll be back by about midday though. Can it wait?"

Primrose suddenly realised that Handel did not look as well as he normally did. His hair was looking a bit dull and his colour was pale. She felt very selfish; she was imposing her problems on these people she had only recently met. Maybe they had their own troubles.

She began to stammer and became very apologetic, stating she had no right to impose upon them. It could wait. She tried hard to mask her fear and confusion and was determined not to let the waterworks overtake her. Her head was swimming with doubt.

The tears tumbled as she turned to head home. Her body shook and her thoughts became dark. She started to feel breathless, as though a belt was tightening around her upper chest. Gasping for air, Primrose reached out for her front door and entered her tortured home. She looked around at everything that had once seemed so well-placed and functional - a mark of order – but now was a mask for disharmony and chaos. How can a home look so well organised and clean, with everything perfectly placed, when all those living within it felt confined and in turmoil? Nothing was where it should be in time or place, despite the picture it presented. Ordered chaos was destroying everything this family had portrayed, not only to others but themselves.

Primrose wrapped herself in a throw rug and cocooned herself in the fetal position. Her pulse slowed as she hid under the layers; and she realised that sometimes, in our darkest moments, we need to retreat from the light of day. She lost track of time. Everything could wait a while until she was ready to face her reality.

She was woken by a door opening, followed by a cool breeze. Primrose heard Annabelle breeze in, humming a pretty tune, followed by another set of footprints and laughter pealing from the kitchen. The two youthful teenagers who swept through her home were full of life and exuberance. Sweet love is bliss - as is ignorance to the harsh reality of adulting. They smiled at Primrose and waved their goodbyes as quickly as their hellos. As long as they saw her alive, they were happy to leave her and get on with their own day. Self-absorbed with a pinch of caring. Some teenagers did not have even that pinch, so she was happy.

Primrose sat up, and a small smile crept to her lips as she felt the affects her new neighbours were having on her family, touching them in a way she never knew was possible. There was something infectious about the Brooks: they were the morning sun creeping up into a clear sky, the clouds shifting on a stormy day so the sun could glisten on the earth below. They were the fresh breeze that allowed everyone to take a deep breath and just smile. They were a little bit wrong - but so right. *Sometimes we don't know what we need. Today I've realised wholeheartedly that what I need is what was once so wrong for me. But now it is perfect.*

Another day had disappeared, yet somehow it felt that it was just what she needed - timeout from the world to readjust and allow herself to accept a new way of living. This was her life, and she would make it one she could be proud of, in every way. Her thoughts and her path had cleared, and she knew that her decisions would now be the right ones - not only for herself, but for all her loved ones who relied on her to make their world safe and secure.

ANNABELLE

For Annabelle, the nights came too quickly. That's when the reality hit her. As she lay in her room in the silence, she thought about her dad in a mental health unit, adjusting to a cocktail of medications that left him in a daze. As he tried to deal with his new harsh reality, Primrose, Annabelle and even little Christian were relaxing into their new life without their dad. Already it was feeling less claustrophobic. They were moving on without him, and Annabelle felt a little guilty. She was liking it all just a bit too much. Life had been so rigid, and there was never any room for a bit of light-hearted living without an agenda or a lesson to be learned.

Each of us is adjusting to a new normal, thought Annabelle, as she stared at the ceiling. Understanding that things will never quite be the same again. For her father, that thought would be heartbreaking. Annabelle knew her mother was still struggling with some inner demons, and while the trauma of the past few days was weighing heavily upon her, she could see a slight lift in her shoulders. She was a strong, independent woman who was more than capable of looking after her family on her own.

Her mother even seemed to be warming to Rae, and that warmed Annabelle's heart. She had found someone who listened to her, made her laugh, and made every moment of each day a joy. She needed this in her life; it was something she had craved and thought was outside her realm. She wanted to respect her parents and make them proud, but not at the expense of her own teenage happiness.

AN EMERGENCY

Next door, the new day started with a bit of a setback. Handel had woken feeling listless and out of breath. Something was not right. He was in-between chemo treatments, and had been feeling pretty well with the help of his pain medication. But he knew his immune system was struggling, so he may have picked something up. He felt tight in the chest and feverish. He had known there would be days when it would be difficult and he would feel like it was all too hard. This was clearly going to be one of them. He turned to his wife and whispered his woes. She reached out in her sleepy slumber and hugged him close. Once her husband's words registered, she made a phone call to Handel's specialist. She was told Handel should go to hospital as soon as possible, and the doctor would meet them there.

Sunnie and Handel were both feeling this disease and its progression; the burdens they were facing were getting heavier to bear, and they were needing all the courage they could muster. A brave face, a few tears and lots of family hugs would help them fight this and deal with it day-by-day. That had always been their strategy, and they were sticking to it.

Sunnie heard footsteps approaching the front door, followed by a short rap. Primrose. Sunnie knew her neighbour was going through a difficult time, and she wanted to support her, but today her own problems needed to take priority. Sunnie usually showed the world her smiles and warmth, but she also had days where the ice-cold reality of life took hold. This was one of those days, and she would just have to let Primrose know. No more than that - some things are best dealt with in private. No need for the whole world to be involved.

"Morning, Primrose! Were you needing something? We are just heading out, but we'll be back later and I'll be happy to chat then. Is it urgent?"

Her heart ached for Primrose, but today Sunnie was needed by the love of her life; the man who made her heart laugh and made each day just a little bit better for herself and her children. *We need this man with his big heart and humility, so today is all about being there for him.* For now, Primrose and her problems would have to wait.

Sunnie helped Handel into 'the beast' - their beautiful, battered but loved old kombi, and waved to Rae and Cee with her biggest smile. She'd told them everything would be OK. They all just had to help each other and live life as normally as possible until this hiccup was over. This challenge, just like any other, would teach them something they had absolutely no idea about before, and they would deal with it no matter the outcome. Life's like that. Every moment we live it, we continue our journey forward. So why not do it with love and laughter? Yes, we will cry and feel immense sadness, but if we do it together and make ourselves a stronger family, we can face anything. Smile a lot - it makes the heart and mind feel just that little bit happier when everything around you is happening at a speed you can't control. *So here I am with the man I love fighting the biggest battle of his life, and I want to make it easier for him. So for now I will smile, love him with all my heart, and hope that the next step is one towards a healthier life for him.*

They arrived at the Emergency Department, and as usual there were people everywhere. Ambulances parked up, people on stretchers, and staff bustling around doing an amazing job. Many people with less serious problems had been waiting for hours, and sighs and grumbling could be heard. Those with life-threatening problems were taken through to waiting doctors quickly. Sunnie approached the triage window with Handel, who by now had an audible wheeze and was finding breathing extremely difficult. His colour was turning grey, and he was extremely weak. A nurse quickly shuffled them behind closed doors, and within minutes the familiar face of Handel's oncologist appeared. He listened to Handel's chest and told them there was a build-up of fluid that needed to be drained off quickly. Once the fluid was removed, Handel would be feeling a lot better, the oncologist reassured them. He would get his registrar to perform the procedure.

Handel gave a weak smile, and Sunnie could see the relief on his face. Just a small stumbling block. Once this was over, they could start stem cell treatment. Then, hopefully, they could put all this behind them and Handel could move on, surfing and soaking up the good life he'd enjoyed before.

An orderly with a happy, smiling face appeared, pushing a wheelchair. He bowed and asked if Handel would accept a ride with him. They all laughed as he gently helped Handel into the chair, and wheeled him off to the ward. As Sunnie turned to go home, she felt the tears welling. Each time he was taken away she feared she may lose him, and the thought broke her heart. She knew she needed to be strong and positive, but there were still moments when doom and gloom shadowed her sunshine.

In the ward, Handel lay with his eyes closed. A clear mask over his nose helped keep his oxygen levels up. The registrar beside him explained in simple language the procedure that would be undertaken. The X-ray had shown the fluid build-up around the right lung; once the tube was in and the fluid drained Handel would feel a lot better, and his breathing would return to normal. A test of the fluid would see whether any infection was present; if there was, it could be treated with antibiotics.

Despite feeling weak and a little beaten, Handel managed a smile. "Anything you need to do, Doc. As long as I get my breath back, I'll be happy."

"You are experiencing a very rare complication of your condition," the registrar continued. "Your oncologist has spoken to you regarding your stem cell transplant. As you have completed your chemo, the next stage of your treatment is now ready. From reading your notes, your stem cell donor has been organised and they are ready to go ahead. Once this treatment has been performed, your immune system will not be as compromised, and within the month hopefully your cell count will be balanced. For now, though, let's get this fluid off your lung."

Handel realised that even though this was a setback, each day meant he was getting a little closer to returning to good health.

A nurse came to his bedside and explained the procedure once more. She helped him feel calm and held his hand as the registrar placed the tube inside Handel's chest. As he watched the blood-stained fluid slide down the clear tubing, Handel felt instant relief. It was all over quickly, but an overnight stay was required to make sure no complications developed.

A night in a cold clinical bed with the background hustle and bustle of a hospital ward buzzing with staff dashing here and there was not really where Handel wanted to be, but he knew it was where he needed to be.

A nurse pulled back the curtains around the bed next to Handel, and he found himself looking into the face of an elderly man with a haunted expression on his face. Muttering to himself, he was attempting to get out of bed, but the nurse gently told him he must stay in bed. She helped him back, tucked his sheets firmly around him and asked if he needed anything. He just ignored her, closed his eyes and settled back into a disturbed slumber once more.

Buzzers, beepers and footsteps all night, soft murmurs of nurses and cries from the sick ... Handel lay sleepless in this sterile unfamiliar environment. *How do people work in this environment? They must be angels sent from above.*

Ever so slowly, light filtered through the window and lights were switched on as the nurses came to do the morning medication round. Smiles and good mornings sounded out as pills were dispensed and the rattling of the food trolley signalled breakfast was not far away. Handel looked up to see a familiar beaming face walking towards him. His gorgeous Sunnie, who always made him feel good, even on his worst days. She leaned over and encircled his neck with her arms, giving him a beautiful smile and kissing him tenderly on the lips.

"Missed you, babe." Sunnie spoke with a song in her voice. They chatted about day-to-day family happenings until Handel's doctor appeared. He was smiling.

"We've decided to move ahead with your stem cell transfusion, so we'll keep you in hospital and get it scheduled in the next day or two. This is a positive step after all your chemo, and means we can soon get your immune system back up and running."

So, the emergency was over - but their next big challenge was not far away.

PRIMROSE

Primrose hadn't heard from Sunnie in a few days. She had been so wrapped up in her own world that she hadn't had the insight to understand that despite her neighbours painting a picture of pure health, sunshine and happiness, they had struggles of their own. So many of us live purely within our own bubble. It is a trap for us all to be aware of. Today though, Primrose could only wallow in the despair of her own desperation. Where was she to turn, if Sunnie did not offer her some hope? The church had been contacting her, offering her support and asking her to come back to the meetings. But how could she? George was in the mental health unit partly because of their advice. Their so-called 'couples therapy' had torn them apart, and she was left with a devastating secret shared with someone she barely knew. Was talking to Sunnie the right thing to do? Her heart said a resounding yes, but if she thought about it logically it made no sense at all. And time was running out.

The sky was changing, and the soft evening light filtered in through her window. Puffy, low-hanging grey clouds were draped in soft sheaths of pink and purple, backlit by the sinking red sun. The world was alive with colour, yet she was sitting blanketed in a storm cloud. She took a deep breath, stood up, grabbed her shoes and walked out into the beauty of dusk. While her husband recovered in hospital, Primrose enjoyed a rare freedom to do as she pleased. Her decisions were hers alone. As the cool evening air met her, a soft wind brushed her face, kissing her gently while she walked and helping to clear a mental pathway to a simpler future. *Life's really not so bad.*

As she strolled down the footpath, her mind slowly emptied and her steps lightened, falling into an easy rhythm. Annabelle and Christian had gone quietly to their rooms with their electronic devices straight after school, as they could see their mother was distracted. Normally she would be on their backs about homework, so they were happy to retreat into their own spaces. The three of them were coping in their own ways to deal with the trauma of a broken father and husband.

Primrose's thoughts were coming at her from all angles, and her brain simply could not put them in any order that made sense. Instead, she grounded herself by focusing on breathing in the cool air and looking around her. The neighbourhood gardens with their neatly trimmed grass, autumn leaves that crunched under her feet, the occasional birdsong - these few things helped her remain calm and allowed her to find some peace and clarity. A few people strolled or jogged past her, walking their dogs, listening to their music, or simply strolling as she was, taking in this beautiful evening with its colourful sky.

As she reached the park, she noticed a male figure sitting with his head bowed, deep in thought. It was Rae. He looked troubled, and his body looked slightly crumpled. Not the usual Rae. He was normally full of light and energy. She stopped in front of him. His eyes were full of tears, and Primrose realised she had intruded. She went to walk away quietly but he smiled up at her and greeted her.

"Hi, Mrs Robins. Not feeling my best at the moment. My mum is at the hospital and I am feeling a bit sorry for myself. I'll get over it. Cee is in the playground. I know I should get her home, but it feels better out here among the trees and the evening sky and other people around. She is happy playing. I shouldn't be brooding, but it's been a tough day."

"Oh Rae, I'm so sorry to hear that. The last time I saw your dad he didn't look very well."

"He'll be OK. He had to go to hospital because of some fluid around his lungs. Now he has to stay in for a bit longer for some other treatment. Not too sure of all the technical terms. Anyway, hopefully it will fix his cancer."

Primrose's face paled. This family had been facing their own crisis while she bombarded Sunnie with her problems, but the gracious lady never once mentioned hers. *How selfish I am! I am supposed to be the good Christian and I simply thought about myself.* For all her criticism of the Brooks' appearance, they had shown far more care to others than she had. *Sunnie did not say a word - she simply listened and supported me. How can I call myself a Christian?*

"Are you OK, Mrs Robins?" Rae looked concerned.

"Yes, yes, I'm fine. Came out for a walk to enjoy the fresh air and pretty evening sky. Annabelle is home studying and Christian is engrossed in a game. Well - I will leave you to it, give your parents my best."

How could I have got so wrapped up in my own head I forgot to ask after others? Life is short. Primrose regretted thinking only of her own gross injustices. How could you keep something as devastating as a life-threatening illness to yourself? It made her realise she had asked very little about her neighbours' life before they arrived next door. She made out as though she was a great neighbour by asking them over to get to know them, and all she did was worry about her own little world and how perfect she needed to appear. *They had asked after us, about our community, our life, but I gave no thought to their situation; that by coming here, they had given up a whole other life – a life I knew nothing about.*

Primrose took a deep breath of cool night air and vowed to change her thinking. She had been conditioned in her own bubble for so long she had become immune to the reality of an outside world where people lived in different and unique circumstances. *I am always telling my children to get off the internet and stop being influenced by a commercial world, but I have been equally influenced – in my case, by the church and their perfect picture of the perfect family home in a nice suburb with my children attending a nice school.* But we don't all have to present ourselves as perfect. Primrose knew she needed to regain her individuality; to stand up for her own values and open herself to a world that teaches us lessons, when we choose to listen. The media simply frightens us or sugar-coats the truth - she wanted to live with authenticity. *Deep thoughts for simply taking a walk to clear my head!* Primrose smiled to herself at her light bulb moment. *Nothing is ever as bad as it seems.*

TAKING CHARGE

Opening her front door, Primrose decided now was the time to make her house became a real home, where every door was open to the possibilities of a fresh new life, and where each person became the unique individual they were born to be.

We need to learn to accept that sometimes good things come from bad situations. At the moment, she needed to accept in her mind what was happening. Her husband was recovering in a mental health unit. Obviously, he had not been facing up to the situation they were both in. They had taken vows to love and honour one another, yet they had allowed others to become involved in a very private world that should have been sacred to them. Their intimacy had been invaded, even though they had been willing participants. They had not been fully prepared for the emotional scars caused by participating in such 'therapy'. George - angry, controlling and under a lot of pressure at work - was disappointed when Primrose no longer wanted to be a willing participant. He had continued to go along to these meetings and was now struggling emotionally with all that went with being intimate outside of marriage, especially after losing her support. It seemed all so wrong.

Primrose wondered how Melissa and Doug were doing. They were the only couple they had truly connected with at the meetings. George had mentioned he found Melissa attractive, and he liked her gentle nature. Primrose still found it confronting that George openly admitted to his feelings. Primrose had kept her feelings close to her heart, and had not uttered a word about the private sessions arranged between herself, Doug and Pastor Neville. Doug was a fireman and had time off during the week, so they had met for discussions with Pastor Neville that led to a few private and intimate sessions between herself and Doug. It was a foreign feeling for her to want to be intimate with, and to feel desired by, another man. Doug was kind and sensitive and they both felt that they were simply following the brief and healing their personal problems. Primrose began feeling again, the emotional numbness was subsiding and she felt she had found a friend who she could trust and who was following a similar journey. Well - that journey had now ended her in extremely hot water. She had started to feel too deeply, which allowed her to see clearly that she was in an unhappy, controlled environment that was rigid and depressing.

But she knew it was wrong, they both did, so they had ended the sessions. Primrose made excuses to avoid the meetings, and George continued to go on his own. He really wanted to find a solution to their problems, and if Pastor Neville's therapy could help, he was going to do whatever was needed. This was George's downfall. Some things just can't be fixed, the cracks are too deep and the damage irreparable. Like their marriage. It made Primrose sad, but she realised they tried too hard to fix something that in the long run would never work. Even if she did believe in God, she realised that ultimately, she was in control of her life and her destiny. Doug had told her he intended to continue going to the meetings as he had found he quite liked the intimacy with others, and had become a little addicted to the voyeurism. That frightened Primrose, and she realised that even within the church congregation there were individuals who were vulnerable to having their moral compass influenced by their so-called leader. Her own husband had been influenced until he became so disconnected, he required intensive therapy.

I must take control of my actions. Today was the day Primrose would decide how she dealt with the situation. She had been told it might take six months for George to fully recover. This gave her time to reassess her own situation; to heal and spend time helping her two children adjust to a totally new life.

We live in a country that allows us freedom of thought, freedom to follow our religion of choice, and freedom to vote. Yet we still have a long way to go until we all have the ability to be heard equally. We are marginalised and defined by our culture, our income, our education and our isolation, due to a globalised economy and an internet that connects us all. But we also have a huge capacity to make big changes if we first dream them, and then live them. Nothing is impossible. With a world that is connected more than ever before, our voices can reach the furthest mountains. We can leave yesterday's mistakes in the past, learn from them, and make the most of the future.

Enough thoughts for now. Time to focus on dinner and the kids. Annabelle and Christian both wandered into the kitchen; the aroma of the sauce simmering on the stove top with all its herbs and spices had lured them from their bedrooms. Nothing like a huge plate of spaghetti bolognaise and fresh bread and salad to bring the family together. Christian was a little quieter than usual, and a bit sulky, which Primrose understood to be due to his dad not being around. Even though George could be cantankerous and strict with his son, they had a deep love. The father and son bond is important, and Christian was missing having his dad there to bounce off about his sport and video game challenges. *I can do motherly and I will do it as best as I can each and every day, so I don't have regrets,* thought Primrose. *Will I do it all perfectly? No, but I will do it with only good intentions.*

The smiles were returning slowly and a small amount of laughter was occasionally sneaking into the conversation, like that one note that makes a melody sing. They had never quite got it right before; they tried too hard and relied on the power of others, instead of making their own music. One note is all it takes to create discord. It may seem small, but its impact is huge. Was it George? Or was it simply their beliefs that needed to change? Too easy to blame others.

Anyway, for now that small amount of laughter was just what Primrose needed to hear. It meant they were healing. Annabelle, with sadness in her eyes but a brave smile on her lips, put her arm around her mother and whispered, "It will all be OK. We just have to let what has hurt us go. Dad will be OK too."

Primrose hugged her with all her heartfelt love and hoped that her daughter still felt that way in six months' time.

Christian chattered on about his day at school. His friend Liam was cheeky to the teacher and was made to stand outside. Cee was given an award for her beautiful story about the seashell that whispered sounds of the ocean to those who needed to hear kindness.

"Cee may be a girl but I like her as much as the boys. She knows so much about the bush and animals. She is everybody's friend. She said everyone needs a friend and we all get sad at times and need someone to sit with them."

Primrose smiled at him as he proceeded to say how sad he was that his dad wasn't around.

"I know he gets grumpy and angry but I love him. I miss him." The little boy looked to the floor and his head drooped.

Primrose swept him into her arms and hugged him tight. "I know it's hard. Dad needs a rest, and when he feels a bit better in a few weeks we will visit him."

Primrose couldn't promise that everything would return to how things were. Life changes, and sometimes what was, may never be again. We would change and grow as a family, and time would continue to move forward, whether they were happy or not. She could only parent and guide her children through life the best she could. As parents, she and George needed to make the choices that would make their children as resilient as possible; those choices would impact how the children would cope with the outside world. They both needed to step up.

She hugged her two precious kids and promised the one thing she knew she could deliver now and in the future.

"I love you both so much!"

RAE OF LIGHT

Rae sauntered home from the park with Cee. The light had dissipated and the darkness was dampening his spirits. The full moon began to shine, reminding him that even in darkness, light guides us. Never allow the mind to take you where you don't want to be. Thoughts become life - keep them just a little wild and carefree so the journey the spirit guides you on is the one you want to dance to. For the journey we choose; the ending remains the same for us all. Smile and love with all your heart. Rae felt a warmth spread through him as he picked up his pace and headed home, where he knew there would be love and laughter despite the health of his dad.

Sunnie was happy to see them both walk through the door.

"Dinner and a board game. How does that sound? Cee, you get to choose the game."

Headbands was Cee's favourite. Soon, Cee was wearing a band stating she was the Queen of England, while Sunnie was Mr Bean, and Rae was Donald Duck. Some light-hearted fun was just what they needed. Life would sort itself out, be it tomorrow or the next day. Right now he was in a happy place where he was free to just chill and relax.

They played until it was time for little Cee to get some sleep. Tucking her in, Sunnie - just as she always did - began a story that came from her heart and soul. Rae had always loved these spontaneous stories, so he poked his head in and listened. It reminded him of when he was young. Sometimes they were stories about how the moon met the stars each night, and how they looked down upon a world filled with magic. Different characters, different messages but always an ending that made you feel happy and content and ready for sleep.

When Cee started nodding off, Sunnie and Rae said their goodnights and went back to the lounge. Sunnie did not want to sit alone tonight. Her worries were taking up too much space. Rae was a welcome distraction, and she wanted to focus on how he was accepting this challenge of his dad being sick.

They grabbed a blanket and sat close, as the night was cool. Sunnie had made hot chocolate. They sipped and spoke quietly about their day, their fears, and the days ahead. Sunnie knew it was tough for Rae, and she did not want him to think he could not shed a tear or express his emotions. He spoke easily; he had always been a kind, caring boy with a logical approach to life. He loved the outdoors, loved animals, yet also loved to physically engage with the world through any kind of sport. She wanted to check in with him - not only how he was feeling about his dad, but how life was.

"So what's been happening at school? Any new friends? I've noticed one that looks pretty special and is close to home!"

Rae smiled. "Yes, that friendship is certainly special to me. Annabelle has been so accepting and inclusive. She has made this move so much easier. She is warm, funny, caring and loves my jokes."

They both laughed, then became quiet and retrospective.

"Seriously though, she is one of the best things to happen to me. Her family are so different to ours, and she loves hearing about the country life and how we chose to live a life of self-pro-vision. She is open to others and their differences, despite her family being extremely conservative. I love that. She is quiet and reserved but confident in her own self. She doesn't follow the pack.

"I have found the whole private school thing to be different, but deep down we all want the same thing as teenagers. To be ac-cepted. They like to teach and preach that love and acceptance are a must and that God guides us through everything we do. I get that we must be loving and caring, but I still find believing in something I can't feel and see difficult."

Sunnie spoke. "Well I've never been exposed to the church, but I know that lots of things we can't see and touch affect us. Our emotions for one. I can't always see your thoughts, yet I see your actions. I suppose we don't always have to see things for them to be believable. We breathe air we can't see, yet our lungs move, so we know oxygen is filling us and keeping us alive. I suppose some people believe God is love, and we see love through actions. We feel and then we act. Love is seen through our actions.

"Your dad is sick. I can't see the cancer, but I can see what it has done to him. I trust the doctors, and their knowledge to heal him. They can't say 100 per cent it will work, but a small percent-age of that may be healed by faith. Our spirit is what I believe oth-ers term God. So if that heals your dad then I do have faith, even though I have never set foot in a church. Then we can go back home to where our heart lies, on our property surrounded by the earth and the sea and all things wholesome.

"That is where his true healing will take place. The salt-tinged air and the sand between his toes, the earth turned and enriched growing our daily food, the birds awakening us each morning with a different song. I miss this each and every day, but in a few months, I know it's where we will be again.

"I have always raised you to believe in yourself and your abilities. You have the power to live a good life and subsequently make others' lives better by your acceptance and kindness. Be someone you are proud of and live in a way that makes you and others around you happy and content. I think that's what the school is trying to teach you, using God as their guide.

"I believe our spirit and our land guide us by providing us with the tools to live well with what we have, heightened by our assistance. If a flower wilts with the heat it is up to us to water it. If we don't, it will die. This is how we make a difference. Everyone has a different spin on life, but deep down we all wish for the same thing. Love and acceptance. Just like you and your friends at school. We also need strength – when it's combined with love and acceptance, we can conquer the difficult times. A bit like we are doing now. We are not alone - everyone has their battles. Some fight them silently and others share their troubles - as they say a trouble shared is a troubled halved.

"Time for rest. Love you, sleep tight, sweet dreams my Rae of light."

GEORGE

The soft hoots of the night owls were the only sound to be heard among the rustling trees. Streetlights dropped golden rays onto the street below, while the full moon glowed brightly, shifting the tides and causing havoc on those fragile souls who tossed and turned with restless minds.

George sat by the window, entranced by the golden orb glowing above the trees in a pitch-black sky sprinkled with diamonds. *When did I lose the beauty and wonder of this vast universe in which we live?* His mind was troubled, and his thoughts would not stop. They would fire rapidly at him, chaotic, sporadic - then there would be nothing. He would find himself staring mindlessly into a vast empty space full of absolutely nothing. It was like he had lost his soul and was floating aimlessly in a vast space, void of anything in touch with life. Lost, alone and with no emotion. He could not keep up with the swing of his moods, like a heavy, out-of-control pendulum with no set rhythm. One moment swinging furiously, then stopping and laconically starting again with little momentum.

His medications had thrown out his body clock. He slept all day, and then when the world stopped and slept, his mind began to race and he found himself alone and once more in the dark-

ness. His thoughts would frighten him. He felt like a child needing comfort from his mother's arms and the glow of a soft lamp
to keep the monsters at bay. Yet no one was here for him. He
had slowly over time pushed everyone away as he got swept into
a selfish journey driven by the materialism of modern society.
He had lost sight of what was important in the pursuit of fine
schools, children who did what they were told, the perfect home
and the perfect family. Hours and hours at work slaving for the
high income had made him into a monster of western society,
and now he was locked away from everything he had been striv-
ing to give his family. Even now with his broken mind, George
knew it was all wrong. He craved what was promised by God –
Eden, the land where the future was filled with peace and love
and like-minded people.

Each day, George was surrounded by nurses, psychiatrists and
psychologists looking to stop the chaos of so many broken minds
that couldn't cope with a world being driven by technology on a
journey no one knew how to control; being driven at such a pace
that it was impossible to keep up with. It was breaking minds and
hearts and leading to fractures that were not able to be healed by
modern medicine.

*Blue pills, pink pills, and a white one too. Add a small orange one
and maybe that will do.* There is no one remedy; it is a matter of
finding the cocktail that suits you. Maybe one that can help you
still the mind and breathe in slowly so that the world does not
whip it back into its hectic pace. Maybe it's a one-on-one session,
or a group session, or maybe some one's story will resonate and
you will make sense of what has caused you to opt out of a world
that stops for nobody.

Here, in this unit, one thing stands out most of all – the need
for these broken minds to be alone in silence. People walked
around with their heads down and a shuffle to their step. Some
of these slow, deliberate movements might have been drug-in-

duced, but when combined with a mind that is confused, depressed, manic or psychotic, it paints a picture of a room full of broken mechanical robots, or birds without wings and a song. They were all injured and unable to fly. Hence the sorrow. The world as they knew it had gone and they no longer knew how they fit in. Change is something that we all find hard, and when the mind has forgotten how to function, change is impossible to handle.

Broken minds in broken bodies quietly sitting in a space they feel they don't own. Despair and despondency, darkened by a deep depression that slowly crept in deep, caused by everyday living in a busy world that left them behind.

That's me. George Robins. A man who had intelligence, love, and a desire to succeed and provide. Somewhere along the journey he got lost, and now he was here where he could only hope that with time, rest and medical help he could recover and return to the routine of a life in which he functioned.

Time moves slowly within these walls, thought George. Slower than the outside world, thanks to the cocktail of medications they were all given to try and treat the chemical imbalances caused by an over-excited brain rattled by the real world. *Now I have some clarity, but it hurts so deep. I look into the darkness for the torchlight of the nurse, who will hand me my relief and put me back into a drug daze so that I can learn to slowly deal with the collapse of my life that I caused, hurting not just myself, but those I loved.* George shuffled back to his bed and waited for the medications to relax his mind. The early morning sun began to creep in through his window as he closed his eyes to the world.

Time and patience is the essence to true healing. George had little patience and too much time. *God has let me down. I trusted those who preached his word and guided me, and now I have been left with nothing.* The medication simply made George's thoughts slow down, it didn't erase them. The psychiatrist wanted him to undergo several electroconvulsive therapy sessions, and follow up with an electroencephalograph. *When will it all end? So many tests with long and complicated names he could hardly say, let alone spell. Simply part of another complicated world he had no chance of understanding in his present state.*

The world went dark as George slipped into a drug-induced sleep where nightmares are magnified. Nude bodies clambered over one another, seeking satisfaction, separated from the ones they loved. Screams of ecstasy and primal lust mixed with a loss of attachment. A room full of people, heightened sexuality, searching and searching. Then everyone disappeared into their lonely suburban lives behind their picket fences, devoid of all emotion, following a mundane existence of work, bills and tiresome duty. A deep primal scream erupted from George as he was woken by a nurse gently shaking him to release him from his torment. He wiped the perspiration from his brow and began to cry. Even sleep could not take his demons away.

The nurse settled George and headed back to the front desk. It was time. She searched for his wife's number and rang it.

PRIMROSE

The phone beside Primrose's bed woke her, and she heard a pleasant female voice introduce herself, speaking with authority.

"Mrs Robins, I'm sorry to disturb you, but we haven't seen you yet, and I am concerned your husband is not doing so well. He may need some family support to aid and speed up his mental recovery. Just a short visit from a loved one can do so much more than all the medical help in the world. It does not have to be a formal visit with a mental health practitioner present, just a quick visit to let him know he is not forgotten. I understand that he was violent with you before he was admitted, but he is now medicated and has shown no violence in the past month. Maybe it is time. The staff will be close by if you need our support."

Primrose was silent. She felt shaken.

"Mrs Robins?"

"I'm sorry, but I simply can't. I've been hurt too badly and I'm just not feeling up to seeing someone that has broken our family into pieces."

"I understand. But George is broken too, and while you are home with your family, he is here fighting his demons with only the medical staff, who can treat the symptoms but not the cause. So maybe if you can find it in your heart to give him ten minutes of your day, if not your forgiveness, he may have some chance of a normal recovery. Think about it."

Extremely distressed, Primrose put down the phone and began to weep loudly. How did she get here? Her husband had always been the family leader, someone with good values who put a roof over his family's head and food on their table each day. Her mother had called him the perfect husband, and to others outside the home that's how he presented. Yet somewhere along the way he became overbearing, controlling, demanding, angry and unreasonable. He demanded perfection and pigeon-holed everything and everyone. Nobody else was quite as good as himself and he put everyone down instead of providing encouragement and love.

Does he realise this is who he has become? He is not the man I married. He presents differently to everyone. How can I not know him anymore? Primrose didn't want to see him, yet she felt an obligation - who else would help him through this terrible time? She had been with him for so long; had always supported him and followed him. *He has made me do things I would never have done with anyone else, and now I am facing my own personal dilemma because of it. I am really in a mess. Maybe I am the one who should be in a mental health facility.* How could she be a good mother while she was so confused? Her children needed her; George must fight his own demons. Primrose had some big decisions to make, and it was getting close to the time she must put a plan into motion. *No. I will not be visiting George anytime soon. My health, my children, my priorities, my choices.*

****

As light crept through the cracks of her louvred windows, sunshine fell like gold across Primrose, lying in bed. As it warmed her belly, she felt butterfly wings gently within. *Another day of manoeuvring myself towards a future that was turning out to be completely different than I would have imagined a year ago*, she thought.

She heard movement in the kitchen. Annabelle and Christian were starting breakfast. Lazy Saturday mornings were when they all just took their time around the kitchen table with toast, bacon, eggs and coffee. The aroma of bacon wafted through the house and Primrose grabbed her gown and headed for the kitchen. She was greeted by two smiling faces as Annabelle poured her a coffee and fetched her breakfast from the warming oven. Primrose felt blessed in so many ways. Some of George's hard-handed Christian ways had made them close, but it had also built walls instead of doors. Her job now was to knock down a few of those walls so that they could open up and talk about the things they had tried to deal with alone. She knew she was still guilty of that, and needed to work on herself. She wanted them all to be able to talk openly, love warmly and trust one another implicitly. To do this, she needed to let them into her world without making her troubles fall too heavily on their young shoulders. *A delicate balancing act.* Primrose had to realise that nothing is perfect; that things will and do go wrong, and that life is a learning curve. Adults make mistakes too.

A gentle breeze carried a peal of laughter from next door, followed by a closing of car doors. Handel was home from hospital, and the kids were heading out early. The laughter reminded her she had a lot to be happy about. She noted the sparkle in Annabelle's eyes as she, too, heard the laughter of someone who had helped her realise that while life has its ups and downs, there is always something to laugh about.

Primrose felt her new neighbours were definitely sent to them with a message. She and her children had all been touched by their carefree spirit. It was impressive how they had adapted to feel at home in a city that was so removed from their love of being at one with nature, and having their souls fed by that which the earth provided. Here in the city, life was complicated by having to deal with more of everything – more people, more cars, more noise, more lights and more choice in everything. But it also provides jobs and entertainment and all the fun things that go along with city life. It could be a good life, as long as you didn't build walls so high around your own little castle that you didn't allow yourself the freedom of living among the hustle and bustle. The butterflies in Primrose's stomach were fluttering as fast as the thoughts in her head. She could barely keep up.

But today was a new day, and some fresh air, a long walk and a chat was just what she needed. It was time to get out of her own troubled headspace and help her neighbour. In her darkest moments, Primrose had come up with a plan.

She felt a little selfish, but her plans for the day did not include her husband. She had thought long and hard, but her Christian heart had hardened, and she just could not forgive him, or the church, for the way they had manipulated and abused her. She had been left with the aftermath of men who had controlled her and left her to suffer. It was unforgivable. She needed to stand up now and be her own person. She was more than capable of making her own decisions and living a strong, independent life. The tragic events of the past few weeks had taught her that she had been controlled for too long. Primrose was not a strong feminist, but she did believe that women needed to teach their daughters to be able to plan their lives to provide for themselves financially. Too many men held women to ransom, with the women unable to leave because of their financial dependence. The gender inequality in wages still exists, but education meant women could earn enough to support themselves and their children if the need arose. Primrose had trained as a teacher, and she was more than capable of returning to teaching while helping her children to a successful future. She could do it on her own – without the lies, the manipulation and deception from those who supposedly were there to love and support her till death do them part. Abuse and control were not something that could be just confessed and forgiven. *George has to fight his own battles, and I no longer will stand meekly by and be used to present his picture-perfect family.*

George's demons were dark and deep; they had grown and festered quietly from a life ridden with guilt from the effects of an overbearing, controlling and angry father. Now here he was, mirroring his father. Primrose felt no pity. *He could burn in hell for dragging me into the depths with him. I will not pity him when he had no conscience about allowing others to abuse me, the one he supposedly loved.* There were no excuses for him making Primrose allow the church leaders to manipulate her into participating in behaviours that were outside her own moral code, even if it was their belief they were helping their marriage. *Where was my common sense? I allowed him to control me and I lost my sense of identity.*

Primrose's thoughts cleared as she showered. Feeling the gentle mound of her stomach, she realised that it was every woman's right to love herself, and to choose who she allowed to love her back. *Respect yourself, and never allow yourself to be manipulated or be with someone that has no respect for you.* She allowed the warm water to slide over her body, cleansing every part of her. With a clear mind and a healthy body, she could face anything.

Stepping out onto the bathroom floor, Primrose looked at her body in the mirror. She was blossoming. This was a time of new growth, in every part of her life. Change was frightening, yet to grow and experience life to the full, we need to be brave and allow new things to develop. *Well, I am certainly doing that in a way I never have before!*

A CONFESSION

Primrose headed next door. She was determined to set her plan into action. Time was running out. Sunnie opened the door with a huge smile and a warm hug; her usual greeting for everyone she knew; a smile that warmed the coldest heart and made you instantly feel like she was your best friend. No hidden agendas, just genuine friendship. A rare trait in city life. *To think I stuck my nose up in the air and pre-judged her and her family in the harshest manner only a month before.* That came from years of being indoctrinated by a church that built people up by filling them with fear. Primrose felt totally disillusioned after growing up believing that all the church did was good. Something about these marriage meetings had not sat well with her from the beginning. Her belief in the sanctity of marriage was so deep she could not believe the church would ever participate in acts that were not in the best interests of Christianity, and Pastor Neville had alleviated her doubts with plausible explanations. George also believed so strongly that she felt she should also believe. But her beliefs were blind, and she followed willingly into what she now could see was a place no true Christian should be taken. Those she loved and trusted the most had placed her in a vulnerable position. Pastor Neville was someone as a family we trusted implicitly. *I thought these things only existed in novels, not real life. How sheltered my existence had been.* 'Hell by the bell' is what she would call it. Church bells ring, drowning out the cries of the vulnerable, while men draped in long gowns and bathed in heavenly light led a congregation hidden within walls of deceit.

"Morning Sunnie! Are you free for a walk? I'd really like to finish our conversation this time, there is so much more to this situation. There is a lot to tell, but I only want to if you are OK with that? I know you have your own challenges at the moment."

"Sure am! Hold on, I will just find my sneakers. Come in."

No one else seemed to be home. Primrose had heard the family's laughter as they all headed out to start their day; Handel laughing the loudest and spreading his usual good spirit. No one would ever know he was battling to save his life.

Courage and strength. Primrose drew on both to support her as she walked and talked, outlining her plan.

"Reflecting on our discussion the other day, and the weight of it, I can understand this may all be pretty confronting. Before telling you, only one other person had heard my confession, and that person was a man that hid behind the robes he wore, manipulating the world to suit his desires. He told me to keep my secret close to my chest and confide in no one. Pastor Neville has always guided our spiritual life and we as a family have always trusted him implicitly. So what I am about to expand on is how myself, George and other members of the church community have been led to believe they are being helped in their marriage when in fact there is a much sinister plan taking place. I think George was made aware at some point and possibly other male members, but I believe all the women have been blindly entangled.

"We have arrived where we are due to a faith that has never faltered. So when trouble stirred within our marriage it was the church we turned to for help. We have always had huge support through our community. They said we were not alone with our issues. So we were told to come along and join the meeting. We were given so much support and were surrounded by others who were floundering due to intimacy issues. Pastor Neville assured us through participating and learning along with others about true intimacy and love we would not only help ourselves as married couples, but our wider community. Others were also finding the modern world a difficult place to manoeuvre and maintain the joy of Christianity.

"Life was leading us down a path of family destruction. It all seemed plausible and I was ready to do anything to help our failing marriage. As the weeks passed and they realised we were committed, the Pastor spent a lot of time alone with the men. George was always quite secretive about what occurred during their time as a group. I simply thought they were discussing things that would help us within our marriage and may be sensitive to us women. Now I realise there was lot more to this than just helping marriages.

"Pastor Neville spoke to me privately after George was taken into hospital. He wanted to put a theory to me, but wanted it to go no further than our walls. It is something only discussed with families of the congregation who had been committed in every way to the church and its beliefs. He was becoming concerned about the modern world, noticing there were a lot more families turning to the church for support due to marriage breakdowns. He felt responsible to help.

"Our church collects a proportion of our wages to commit to causes the church believes in. He had discussed a particular investment briefly with some of the men at the meetings. George was one of those men. It was important they were fully invested and there was to be no discussion outside of the meeting.

"But since George has been in hospital, his payments have stopped. Pastor Neville was concerned and wanted to know if we were both still committed to the cause.

"George had never shared with me about the private meetings or what the men had discussed, so I was completely blindsided by what Pastor Neville told me. Apparently, we have invested in some land, isolated from the city, and it is the church's plan to create a community that will be untouched by the modern problems that are creating a breakdown in our families.

"This place, known by only a few, is where children of God can grow and thrive away from outside influences. Pastor Neville told me that it's like the Garden of Eden, where no evil can touch them. These children of God will grow up to become our leaders, and continue our work in the church. They guide those of us who are influenced by the modern world.

"Pastor Neville said to me, 'You were troubled by the modern world and so we have chosen you to procreate and renew connections, providing us with the fruit that will allow our teachings to continue without bad influences passing onto the next generation. The funds raised from the congregation have purchased this rich fertile earth to provide for those with the vision of living a pure life, so that they can attain a higher level when they ascend into the purity of heaven in the afterlife.' What he was telling me is that by procreating with those within this community, precious little angels are born to create heaven on earth. He told me that I had been chosen to give this gift to the cause, and that I could count myself among the highest ones."

It was a long speech. Sunnie listened. She had no words – yet.

"So it seems George was aware of all of this, yet chose to leave me in the dark." Primrose was in full flow now. "Did he hope that we would one day have a child that would be seen to be a 'divine one' of God? I believe he may have, but was grappling with the consequences.

"Now I realise I have been manipulated. I am pregnant with a child the church will deem one of their 'angels'. So it is important to me I keep my pregnancy completely secret."

"Does George know you are pregnant?" Sunnie's concern was real.

"I haven't told him. I was already concerned with what was happening in our marriage. Then when his mental state started to deteriorate, I was frightened by his behaviour. I didn't know where to turn. I had no idea of the church's views until Pastor Neville came over for dinner and enlightened me about Eden.

"I need to protect not only myself but others that have become entangled in this manipulative, deceptive, deranged world. I know I can't do it alone. I have come to realise that the idealism of the church was akin to brainwashing, and it's possible that Eden is a cult.

"Sunnie, I need to protect my children. As for George, I think he may have been torn between the moral obligations to his family and the church leading him down a path that ultimately destroyed his sanity. He had kept the secret and I think was just waiting for me to add to this world with a 'gift' approved by the high and mighty. He had been brainwashed that we should become a part of something pure and he wanted desperately for his family unit to escape the devil's work. Eden was the new way, and George was going there, but he wasn't sure how he could convince me and the children to join him. Now George has lost everything, through believing he would become part of a better world. He has lost his job, his family and finally his mind, yet he still believed that the path he followed would ultimately provide for and protect his family."

Primrose was confiding to Sunnie more than she thought she would. But she trusted Sunnie more than anyone she had previously trusted. So she continued.

"I am now alone without George and the support of the church. I need to make sure that no one becomes aware of my pregnancy. I believe the families that have disappeared from our church have also been manipulated, and that they are in this place they name Eden, a community unknown of and separated from our main church community. George obviously wanted us to become a part of this new world. Our friends Melissa and Doug left just recently, telling us that they were relocating to get their marriage back on solid ground.

"Now I believe this is what they were told to tell others within the church, and they moved to Eden, entangled in this new church society."

Sunnie was shocked, but listened to Primrose with a tenderness and warmth that emanated from a deep love, a love that had been nurtured from childhood, in the belief that all those who plant their toes into the earth are equally deserving of compassion. This story she had just listened to seemed to have come from the darkness of rotting, twisted minds. Layers of lies, fabricated to create a world of fantasy by those determined to destroy society, while preaching they are men of God. *Why do we continue to divide and remove ourselves, when to create harmony, we just need to come together?* Sunnie's understanding of Christianity is that we should all love one another and accept our differences, for they are what make us special. But this situation is real, it's complicated and it is destroying a family. There is nothing loving, kind or compassionate here. It is the exploitation of good people's vulnerability in a time of conflict, by instilling false love and hope.

Sunnie realised her neighbours had hit rock-bottom. We all crave love, peace and harmony. George and Primrose felt that by losing intimacy they had lost everything. In the name of the church, they were led to lust, desire and perversion by those they trusted, and now were facing the destruction of their marriage. The head of their perfect Christian family is now broken in mind and spirit, living in an isolated world that he cannot find the strength to escape without the medical intervention of man-made drugs.

Sunnie knew she must decide how much she was willing to invest in this new friendship. Her decisions would not only impact on her, but Sunnie's whole family. She has helped friends out through difficult times before, but nothing like this.

Thoughts whirled through her mind like a freight train. *I need to respond and make it heartfelt without undermining my family. I want to help, but this is heavy.* Annabelle and Christian – both delightful, well-mannered, intelligent children albeit with very controlled emotions - had become close friends with Rae and Cee. Sunnie had raised her children to be respectful of others, yet to hold their own opinions, express their emotions openly and share their warmth affectionately with others. Her decision would impact them all. *I can't make such a huge decision without a family meeting,* she thought. *This discussion needs to go beyond me, it's something we all need to understand.*

"Primrose, I am in shock at the moment. I am so sorry you have had to go through this." She hugged her friend tight and wiped the tears from her cheeks. "But this is huge, and I can't keep this from Handel and the kids. So if you need me to keep this a total secret I can't be involved. If I can be open with Handel and the kids, we can tackle this together. Handel is nearing a turning point and is doing well, so our return home is looking like it may be closer than we thought. But if you need a peaceful place that is remote, tranquil and away from the stresses, we may have the answer. Let me discuss it with them this week, and I will let you know."

Primrose openly wept; her body wracked by huge sobs. Her legs gave way, and Sunnie supported her to a park bench.

"This is too much for one person to bear, you really need to confide in a professional. They can be impartial and help you understand the emotions you are going through."

Slowly, Primrose took a few deep breaths. "Thank you." She suddenly felt less alone, as if a huge weight had been lifted from her shoulders. The emotional turmoil along with her ever-changing hormones had caused a tsunami of emotions to be released.

****

It was going to be one very long week. The details of her future journey would need fine-tuning. Primrose knew that any minute detail, if not perfect, could cause a catastrophic avalanche of human despair and grief. Her body was changing as quickly as her mindset, but the truth must be told. She had thought she could simply do as other families had done, and mysteriously disappear, but Pastor Neville had chosen the wrong woman this time. She simply would not disappear. When Primrose thought about all the families in their church who had moved, she could count at least fifty over the last decade. Had they all helped create this village of children who were being groomed for a life within the boundaries of this religious realm? Who is guiding them and where do they live? *Do I even want to know the answers to these questions? I may put my family and friends at risk if I expose the church's hidden world.*

Each day dragged into the next. Primrose's mind and body were exhausted. She still had not had the strength to go the hospital to see George. Was his mind destroyed from the burden of his knowledge? Is this what tipped him into the dark depths of depression and anger? To keep a secret like this locked in your mind is a certain path to mental illness. He was a good man with good intentions, yet his mind had been manipulated when he first confided in the church over their loss of intimacy. *How could he lie to me like that? How could he place me in such a vulnerable position, knowing that, like him, I was trying to help our dwindling relationship?* It made Primrose question George's love. Her maternal instincts were strong, despite the dark complexities of the conception. There was no way she would allow the church to manipulate her and take her family to Eden. *No one has that power over me, not even a church that believes it is the highest power on earth. They are deluded and the truth needs to be exposed.*

Difficult times never last forever. Primrose was certain that a resolution would be found, and she needed to instigate it now. How many others are at this moment in the same situation? Pastor Neville had always told them to stick to those within their church; to only make superficial friendships with outsiders. They didn't belong in their godly community, not until they had proven through church attendance and community commitment that they were ready to belong. Primrose understood they were building a life for the church's future leaders – literally, from the seed up - away from the influences of a world that has lost human contact. From love they would grow love, and spread it from one to another. If this 'love' resulted in pregnancy, then the child had been chosen by God, and belonged in Eden among the other chosen ones, learning how to lead the church into the future.

Not on Primrose's watch.

THE BROOKS

Sunnie prepared a meal of dishes the family all loved. She had found a farmers market selling beautiful fresh produce; they liked to know exactly where their food had been grown, and they loved to support those who worked the land to grow it. This family dinner would involve some serious discussion that they needed to all be a part of. Cee would be affected by this, but despite her tender age she needed to understand what was happening, and how it must go no further than their family, and the family next door.

She was reluctant to put this on Handel at the moment, but it could be a welcome distraction from his own precarious situation. The doctors had given him good news; his tests showed him to be in remission. They had made this city move to show the children another side to life; little did she know that evil could hide behind good, and she would be asked for such help after a simple knock on her door. Yet, as life had shown her over the years, you never quite know when life can tip you upside down and shake you to the core. It just takes time to climb back up again.

As they held hands to thank the earth for providing them with this meal, Sunnie spoke.

"The earth provides us with what we need only with our own help. If you want reward, you need to do the groundwork and feed the earth the nutrients it needs to thrive. People are the same. We have recently made new friendships that the universe has asked us to nurture. Today I have been trusted with a secret that I now must share with you, my closest loving humans. It must never escape the walls of our home, for it could destroy lives and it is our place to help when we are needed. I need to know that if I share this with you all, you are happy to keep the secret."

Handel, Cee and Rae placed their right hands to their closed lips. This meant it was a secret that comes with no malice; it was simply a seal of silence due to love. No secrets other than these were allowed to exist in their family; it was one of their many family codes that were instilled to bring pure harmony and love.

"So now that I have everyone's seal of silence, please be prepared to be just a little bit shocked at what I am about to propose.

"I have only recently learned of these tragic actions, and I'm trying to look at the positives and how we may help. I am not lingering on the moral aspects and the criminal injustice of it all, as we as a family are in no way involved in this dark side of life.

"Whatever we decide, it will affect all of you, so I want you to all listen carefully. Cee, you are very young and I don't want to burden you with adult problems. You only need to understand what might change and how it will affect you.

"Handel, I hope you will approve my holding this family meeting before I have confided in you. Life has had its challenges for you of late, and I didn't want you dwelling on others' problems. Rae, you are mature beyond your years and I trust you will make your own decision with a clear mind and an understanding of a world that is far from perfect, but still remains beautiful."

Three pairs of clear sparkling blue eyes looked straight at Sunnie with wonder and intrigue. *How will they look at me after I divulge the content of what I am about to propose?*

"I'll try to put it to you slowly, but it will shock you, and change our lives if we decide to help the ones in need. It involves our neighbours. All of us have become close to someone next door. I have grown to see the kindness and vulnerability in Primrose, Rae has seen the beauty and purity in Annabelle, and Cee has found a lovely friendship and playmate in Christian. Handel hasn't had the time or been well enough to get to know George, made even harder by the fact George hasn't been around for a while. He has been unwell, and is currently in a mental health facility. What I am about to tell you will shed some light on why.

"Sadly, most families have a dark secret they feel they cannot share, but usually it inevitably catches up with them. Hiding such things can cause them to grow more and more sinister - everything needs an outlet. That's why our rule has always been to share your troubles, and if you are not comfortable with something, talk to someone you trust. Today, Primrose chose that someone to be me.

"So now, I will share with you the dark secret she shared with me. It starts with their church being a place people go to for advice and help in times of trouble, when they need to know it will go no further. Primrose and George had been having some marriage problems, and they turned to the church. It turned out others were facing similar issues, so the Pastor, seeing a need, came up with a plan. He thought that the world had become a selfish, self-obsessed place where everyone wanted instant gratification and communicated through digital devices. He believed it to be hell on earth. So he decided to create his own community that existed in isolation from what he believed to be the sinister influences of the modern world.

"He began Wednesday night meetings at the back of the church. Troubled couples met and group sessions were held to bring back human touch and communication through intimacy. The problem was that to continue with these sessions, it was encouraged that you experiment with others. It worked, as each of them found the intimacy of another stimulating and new. Along with this interaction, the women were told to stop taking contraception, as it played havoc with hormones and was unnatural. The minister believed that the grassroots of today's problems were things like artificial intelligence, and the artificial food and pills people fuelled themselves with. He told the couple that they needed to stay connected, to open their minds and bodies to others that followed the church, and together they would create their own perfect world with babies made through these connections. Because the fathers of the babies conceived at these meetings were often unknown, due to the group interaction, the Pastor was to be known as the father.

"Unfortunately, Primrose is now one of these new mothers. She has not yet told the church, she has not even told George. She doesn't want her child taken away, or her family having to move to this secret place called Eden. She has told no one but me. She wishes to keep it quiet, and to move with us when we head back home. Just until the baby is born. It's a huge, tangled, complicated mess, but she realises that if her life is to go on, she must escape from the clutches of the church and their idealistic society. Primrose believes that George may have known of these plans for their future, and the stress added to his breakdown. She doesn't want Annabelle and Christian to get swept into this world and live in seclusion in a society ruled by a minister who clearly suffers from delusions. He takes pleasure in exploiting people with troubled relationships, manipulating them into his 'meetings' where he gains personal pleasure from observing and being a part of their intimacy. Ultimately, he takes control of the families and their lives.

"As you can imagine, Primrose is distraught, pregnant, and hasn't known who she could trust. We have been asked to help, but I need to know that as a family we can handle what we are about to become involved in. It's obviously very complicated, and will need a lot of secrecy and planning. I need to know you are all prepared for the unknown."

She paused. The silence was heavy; all eyes were on her and Sunnie could see they were all processing what she had told them, within the limits of their age and understanding and the context of their relationships with Annabelle, Christian and Primrose. Shock, horror and disbelief were obvious, along with an underlying sadness for the events that had placed this family, which they had become close to in a short period of time, in such a horrible predicament.

Handel broke the silence by pushing his stool out from the table and moving towards his wife with his arms wide open. 'You, my lovely, are the one to whom others reach out to when they need comfort and warmth. Our sunshine. Primrose does not need her fake God when she has you so close to her heart. How shocking that their trust in human nature has been shattered by those they sought to give them comfort. I am willing to support her in any way we can, as I believe that others are sent to us to not only give us love, but to teach us life's important lessons. Not quite sure I like the lesson here, but I am with you all the way. We came here with an open mind and heart, and we have unexpectedly been touched by the evil side of life. But don't let us forget the evil is outweighed by the good. That is why we have a justice system. This man will pay, but our first priority must be to protect the innocent ones who have been hurt."

Rae had a tear in his eye. He felt crushed by disappointment. No wonder Annabelle had a look of sadness in her eyes, in times of silence, when she thinks no one is watching. He was drawn to her because of this, and her unknown story is one he wanted to become more familiar with, and become a part of, so they could create some laughter on the wind instead of sadness.

Cee sat with her eyes wide open, her heart on her sleeve. Christian had become her all-time best buddy, and all she could understand was that someone had been horrible and made her friend feel unhappy. His dad was sick, and his mum was all alone. She knew that when someone was feeling down, a smile and a hug could make all the difference, and kindness was something everyone deserved. So her plan was to be the one person to put a smile on Christian's face tomorrow at school. Like mum and dad always say - small things make a big difference.

GEORGE

George sat alone by the window. The late winter sunshine streamed through large glass doors, and the garden danced with colour as it touched everything in its sight. Yet George could not feel the warmth, or see the beauty in front of him. Despite weeks of therapy, pills and care, his world was still covered in darkness. He felt overcome by foreboding thoughts of doom due to the damning way the modern world was stealing his family away from God and everything he wanted for his family. Primrose had withdrawn from him, despite him trying to rekindle their love the way Pastor Neville had suggested. Nothing was lifting this heavy cloud, and his whole body felt weighed down by responsibility and the knowledge he had neither the strength nor desire to do anything to change it.

Where are his loved ones now? Not one of them had been to see him in the weeks he'd been here – or was it months? George had lost all sense of time. He no longer felt part of the real world. He got an occasional nod from a fellow patient, and the nursing staff were full of smiles and encouraging words, but somehow they seemed sugar-coated, full of a positivity that he had no need for or understanding of. He stared out the window. He needed to escape this jail, find his family and get them to Eden, where he knew life would be lived as it should be. To George, the real world had spun out of control. Pastor Neville had promised that George and Primrose would find paradise once they rekindled their love with each other and their community. Only then could they enter Eden as a family and contribute a pure child untainted by the outside world. *Why couldn't Primrose just have followed his plan, and trusted him that it would make the family whole again?*

George's mother had always told him that we are all a little broken; the cracks are simply little imperfections that allow God's light to seep in. Well, his cracks had caused an earthquake. The earth could no longer sustain modern existence. Wasn't it their duty to change the path of the world? George was simply trying to save his family, and now here he sat shrouded by doom and darkness, angry at a world that caused suffering to his family. *No wonder people talk about hell on earth. Nothing good about today as far as I can see.* George's eyes were open, but all he could see was darkness, surrounded by people broken by a world they were too fragile to endure.

Darkness and light, day and night, stars and sunshine. All shared a beauty, just in different ways. Even though the stars may not shine every night, they are still there. We can either choose to see only the blackness, or look to the night skies and know that once the clouds clear, the stars will be ours to see. It's all in how we choose to view the world.

LAUGHTER ON THE WIND

Cee left the house knowing that her friend Christian needed her kindness today more than ever. She walked beside him on their way to school, as Rae and Annabelle walked behind them. She took his hand in hers and called out to him to run with her. "Winners are grinners!" she yelled, as the two youngsters took off and left Annabelle and Rae behind. She giggled as she felt her hair blow softly over her eyes as the warm wind touched her face. Christian ran beside her. His pulse raced and his face became flushed. Cee felt good. She'd helped her friend feel the laughter on the wind. She had touched another with kindness. Small things matter.

Rae watched and understood the laughter as he, too, had been guided by his parents and knew that by making the day start out with a shared lightness, the whole mood can change. For Annabelle, seeing her little brother running and laughing was enough to allow her day to feel a bit lighter. She knew things had changed the day the kombi van pulled up next door and the Brooks had tumbled out full of laughter and energy, magnifying the foreboding spirit that had settled in their home and making the already strict routine feel like they were living in never-ending darkness. Her father's mood had gone from sombre and quiet to angry and controlling. Her mother avoided him and when a discussion became an argument, she simply walked away. They had lost communication. and happiness seemed to have walked out the door.

Little did Annabelle know then that her father would end up in a mental health facility and her mother would be left alone to fend for the family. The mood of the house held dark secrets that weighed heavily upon all of their shoulders. But she did have someone next to her who she knew would listen and lighten her day. So she smiled at her little brother and took in the world around her. The sun was shining, and a gentle breeze blew the scent of jasmine towards her; a scent she would now always associate with laughter. Her shoulders loosened as she realised others were the key to helping her through her troubles. She would be OK.

Both Rae and his little sister realised that neither Annabelle nor Christian had been told of the new baby. The two of them held a big secret, and they had to hold it close to their hearts. If it was exposed, it could ruin the whole plan and place a whole family in a dangerous situation. But they had talked with their parents about how they could help their friends. They could be the stars in someone's dark sky simply by reminding them that the clouds will disappear once the wind blows. They could be the laughter that turns the wind, shifting the clouds and leaving the lingering melody of laughter.

DECISION TIME

Handel and Sunnie had the house to themselves. It was decision time; they needed to delve deeper into finding a safe and permanent solution to Primrose's delicate and dangerous situation. Handel spoke with a look of deep thought upon his face.

"This situation, if we get involved, goes much deeper than one family. It's about possibly exposing a cult, an abusive culture within a huge organisation respected by many. The ramifications will spread far and wide. Our lives have always been about living as one with nature, respecting the earth and every living thing. We removed ourselves from city life to enjoy the elements without the huge influence of consumerism and its disregard for the environment. That was the right choice for us. I have nothing against city life and city folk, as they provide jobs and services and provide wealth so that we can all maintain a good standard of living. We moved here primarily to get my health in order and give our children a taste of the big smoke, and suddenly we find ourselves mixed up in a morally corrupt, religious-based drama that could make a TV series. Really! What are the chances! I suppose if I look at it through another window, I see an opportunity to help someone escape a narrow-mindedness that has kept them behind their white picket fence, living a restricted, unsatisfying life indoctrinated by a church mentality.

"So – after that rant - where do we start?" Handel laughed. Not that the situation was funny, but because right in this moment he could choose to laugh or cry, and laughter had always helped him see the bright side.

Sunnie smiled. "As I see it, we have no choice but to help. I would like to quietly set the wheels in motion. Now that your chemo treatment has finished and you are in remission, we can plan to get back home. I think we should move Primrose, Annabelle and Christian safely to our property. It seems this church community has lost quite a few families, but nobody has raised any suspicions. They just assume people move on. So we should be able to move the family without anyone raising questions.

"The biggest problem will be George, once he recovers. No one knows Primrose is pregnant, so she has protected herself from being forced to live in Eden for now. George has been hoping for a pregnancy and wanting to move to Eden ever since Pastor Neville spoke to him about it, once he was sure he had George on side as a true convert. He used the intimacy shared among the group to slowly introduce them to his secret world, where no one would suffer modern-day problems. They were brainwashed and abused when they were at their most vulnerable.

"So we need to do this soon, with precision and a plan that is flawless. Once George has recovered, we will monitor whether he will choose his wife and family over Eden. Hopefully after months of psychiatric help, his mind set will have changed. Then we can go to the authorities and expose the minister's cult once and for all. No one has ever divulged where this place exists, so we have no idea of the numbers we are dealing with. We move Primrose and the children back with us. No one at Dangarup will meddle in our private lives, and we haven't been in the city long enough for anyone to even know we've gone. We have been too busy with our own family to have become part of the community. The church will have no suspicion of anything untoward - Primrose has decided to tell them that due to George's illness, she is taking herself and the children on an extended road trip to clear their heads while George recovers. She has no fixed itinerary and will just go where the wind takes her; she wants to completely change her lifestyle from rigid and routine-driven to something completely out of character. Her busy schedule has led to her family breakdown, and she wants the freedom to get back in touch with her children. They just need time – and so does George.

"I am not sure the church is doing anything legally wrong; they are all consenting adults, and there is nothing wrong with marriage counselling and group therapy. There is also nothing wrong with setting up a community that believes in raising children within the church's beliefs, away from the influences of modern technology. The secrecy of the location and removing themselves and their children from their communities is also not illegal - the only wrongdoing is if it is being done forcibly without their consent. I think Pastor Neville is convincing the men to take control of their families and is manipulating the situation so that they dominate the outcome once the wife becomes pregnant. As the baby is out of wedlock, Pastor Neville tells them that the only way they can live as a family without shame is to become a part of their own community - Eden. He convinces them that it is modern society that has caused their marital woes. But it is him – he is the perverted one gaining his own satisfaction by involving himself and hiding behind the church. The whole organisation makes me sick to my stomach, but I don't think they can be charged with anything illegal. While George has obviously been hiding a lot from his family, I think ultimately, he only ever wanted to save his family during a difficult time."

Handel considered his wife's words. "You're right. We need to meet with Primrose and work through the finer details so that her leaving will not be considered suspect. Maybe a six-month stay while George is recovering, to give them all some breathing space. That way the baby can be born and Primrose can decide what is best for them all. She is going to need income as George's sick leave will not go on forever. So many big decisions to be sorted out. Pastor Neville must not suspect anything, as he believes every child conceived within these church meetings belongs with his community in Eden. Primrose would be expected to just give the child over like everyone else and live within the community.

"Maybe we could also possibly have a quiet chat with this minister, or pastor, or whatever they call him, to put him in his place and shut this 'marriage counselling' group down once and for all – or as he calls it, the 'Follow your Heart' meeting group. Disgusting, degrading and demoralising is what I would call it. He has taken free love and open marriage and turned it into a manipulative act to create a God-obsessed cult that removes and excludes. Free love should be about bringing people together in unity, not segregating. I am not against loving freely, but I am against anything that creates segregation and isolation."

"There are a few ways we can tackle this problem," said Sunnie. "We can't go to Pastor Neville and get angry, as it may spoil any hope of getting Primrose and the family out of the church's clutches.

"We need to brainstorm and come up with an outcome that is good for every single member of that family. Ultimately, it would be lovely if George recovers and removes himself completely from the church and they unite as a family. Can that happen?"

Listening to his wife, Handel 's face became awash with worry. His family meant everything to him and he loved being surrounded by laughter and positive energy. He could face any challenge with a positive outlook. That had been proven over the last few months, as he and his family had stared possible death in the face, moved to a new house, he had survived invasive medical treatments - and they were still happy and laughing and learning about life. Next door, life was lived in a completely different manner and they had splintered into so many pieces. Was it possible for it all to turn out for them? There was going to have to be some radical changes and big moves made to make that possible.

He made an effort to smile at his beautiful wife. "Anything is possible when Sunnie is by your side! Let's see where the wind takes us. With good planning should come good outcomes."

Their biggest obstacle was Pastor Neville, to whom Primrose had confided all her fears to over dinner at her home. He was the only other person that possibly suspected that a new little life was on the way, which would be born out of wedlock in a sinister environment that he manipulated.

"Let's go for a drive to the beach," suggested Handel. "No more talking until our thoughts have been put in place. Clear the congestion and let nature purify the air we breathe so we can think with clarity."

HANDEL AND SUNNIE

Salt air wafted through summer's first breeze, and they felt blanketed and warmed by the afternoon's clear blue skies. The kombi rattled along a coastline edged with homes all fighting for a glimpse of the Indian Ocean.

The sea lifted their spirits, allowing them to lighten and run wildly along the shore, cooling the heat from their inner turmoil. Their lungs filled with clean air that had captured the salt as it drifted wildly over the ocean before gently kissing their faces, connecting them to where their hearts should settle. Slowly their pulses settled as the rhythms of the waves settled their racing minds. This was where they find their inner peace; where problems that seem to be as hard and as high as mountains disintegrated into the grains of sand washed by the ocean's water.

Handel and Sunnie strolled barefoot, with the waves lapping at their feet, the wind behind them and the sun warming their faces. The magic of the seaside saturated their busy minds. Seagulls scattered the sky, beach towels scattered the shore, and children scattered everywhere, playing along the shoreline. As they slowly walked and talked, everything else moved into the background. Somehow all the troubles of the world seemed to be lifted with the sea air that drifted out across the expanse of blue ocean, meeting the horizon in a blue-grey haze. They knew that as long as we all keep rising each day with the sun, there was hope and a new perspective, be it a different hue, shifting sands or a drifting, cloud-dotted sky. How we changed things for the better was the bigger question. With logic, emotional intelligence, and a lot of support. Planning, common sense and attention to detail all help, along with a little bit of time away from the problem to gather your thoughts.

The afternoon faded as a burning tangerine sun sank into the horizon, catching fire briefly as it fell into the sea. *Each day we are held to this earth by a force much greater than us*, thought Sunnie. *We witness such beauty as the galaxy orbits around us, yet we continue to sweat the small stuff.* They both breathed deeply, their sighs melting into the evening sky as they watched nature again painting the colours of our forever-changing world.

Handel and Sunnie had cleared their minds, and they believed they had created a plan everyone could live with. It was time to sit down with Primrose and get this plan in action.

The night air began to wrap itself around them and they both felt chilled. They were quiet on the ride home, giving each other space. But once they walked into the house, the family chatter started. The kids were eager to find out what was on the dinner menu. Cee was getting weary and keen to eat before heading to bed for a bedtime story. Sunnie had thought ahead and prepared a meal before they left this morning, and began heating it. Rae was a little quieter than usual. Handel took him aside after dinner. "You up for a quick card game?"

"Of course dad, I beat you every time." The cards came out and the usual banter started between the two of them. The conversation soon became a little more serious when Rae raised his concern for Annabelle and her family. He wanted to know how they could help them without causing any harm.

Handel was open and honest, explaining that as of yet they had not come up with a definitive plan. They somehow needed to know more about Eden and its workings. With George so mentally unstable, they had no idea about the extent of his involvement with what they could only think of as a cult. Handel told his son that he was considering a visit to Primrose, to have a quiet chat and try and shine some light on how and where they might be able to help. Rae thought a visit from him to Anabelle might also prove helpful. Sunnie arrived then, with herbal tea for them all. With Cee settled in bed, perhaps now was a good time to have a chat with Primrose?

Primrose was more than happy to head over, and Rae would go in the opposite direction to keep Annabelle company. Ten minutes later, the three adults sat down quietly to plan their strategies. Primrose settled into the sofa opposite Handel and Sunnie, sipping at her herbal tea. Once again, she was reminded of how easy and relaxed this household was, with soft soothing music playing in the background and incense infusing the air with a touch of rose. Handel was lying across the wide soft couch in his relaxed-fitting pants and cotton shirt, his hair still tousled from the stroll along the beach. Sunnie had her legs gently resting over his. She was eager to get this discussion started.

"First, what do we do about George?" she began. "He is the one who knows the inside story and the inner workings of the church, as well as the creation of Eden and its location. Somehow, we need him to talk and spill the secrets, so the plans can be exposed - or at least allow Primrose to escape the trappings of this underworld."

Handel spoke up with a firm but loving tone.

"George is carrying the heaviest load, so we need to help him get rid of the trash so that he can see that life can be full of richness without the trappings of the heavy roles we choose to conform to, and the pressures modern society presents us with. He has reached out to a group that created an outlet in a way that had him believe in a power higher than yourselves. We need him to believe we create our own higher power by choosing to live outside the constraints of the mainstream. He has a dark soul, trapped by secrets and conformity. We need to help him understand that his darkness is what is trapping him, not his family.

"It's not going to be easy. So my plan is let him open up to those he trusts and loves the most in this world - Annabelle and Christian. I could take them to the hospital. They go in alone and we get Annabelle to steer him where we can get some answers. Once we know who is driving the community of Eden within the church, we can out-manoeuvre them."

When Handel paused, Sunnie gently eased in with her ideas. "Yes, I agree we need to persuade George. Though from what Primrose has told me, George is in the depths of a deep depression. That is not something easily lifted until the doctors have rebalanced his brain chemistry. He is beyond sunshine, fresh air and a good dose of love and humour."

Primrose spoke then. "I feel so guilty for not wanting to be around George, but he has been a controlling force in my life for too long. I cannot forgive him for being so cruel and manipulative and allowing other people to use their sick sexual desires to involve me, who he supposedly loved with all his heart."

Handel reassured her. "This is all so wrong. Somehow, they have brainwashed George. There are stronger forces here than just church practices. With his medication now a little more balanced, and while he is still less agitated and in a safe environment, I think we just may be able to get Annabelle to pry some vital information from him that may help us understand how all this began. So, I suggest the first step is for Annabelle to visit George, and I am happy to take her. Maybe Christian would be better visiting with you, Primrose, on another day."

A VISITOR

George sat in his favourite corner, isolated from everyone. He had no desire to become friends with these broken pieces of humanity. He may be living in darkness due to the world and its obsession with self, but he knew the light existed. He just needed to escape and create a new life to add to Pastor Neville's perfect community. Then light would surround him again. They could feed him every pill known to man, but he knew the only treatment he needed was to get his family away from the modern world and produce a child untainted by technology and the breakdown of the family unit.

Yet despite sharing the love as Pastor Neville had advised him to, he had been unable to provide the seed to allow the beginning of this perfect new life. Once again, he had failed. He had failed his wife, his children, and now he could not even please the church. This was the story of his life. He could never meet the expectations of those close to him, and now here he was, sitting in a corner, hopeless and alone with no one who cares, not even his family. He dropped his head to his chest and closed his eyes. He had become his own father. The only difference is he had torn his family apart without abusing alcohol. He had sworn never to drink but he did not realise his past had made him controlling and abusive in another manner. There was a gentle tapping on his shoulder. *Not another pill,* he thought. George slowly opened his eyes, raising them without expectations. He could barely believe it. It was his daughter.

"Annabelle?" His whisper was hoarse; he had barely spoken for months.

"Yes, dad, it's me." George stood to hug her, wobbling on his feet. Annabelle was shocked at his frailty. He had become a shadow of himself. He even sounded different.

"Please let me look at you. It seems like an eternity. I have missed you so much. I am so sorry, Annabelle." Tears ran down his face as his eyes cried out for forgiveness.

Annabelle's heart cried silently. She still held so much resentment for the harsh way her father had treated them for so long, and knowing now of what he had planned to do left her little room for forgiveness. She was here to do a job, she reminded herself, and she needed to use her head.

"It's OK, dad. I'm here now. We've all missed you. Maybe we could take a moment to pray that our family can once more become whole."

She noted the glimmer of hope in his eyes. Together, they dropped their heads and held hands, just like they had always done each night at the family meal table. Silence surrounded them and, just for a moment, George felt the familiarity of home. His heart beat faster and his body felt warm. Prayer and family - to him, this was his world. Somewhere, though, it had become distorted. His mind had become as twisted and gnarly as a burned tree, isolated after a devastating bushfire. Among a landscape of black and grey, the fire had consumed him and left him with nothing. Sinking into a dark hole of despair was his only protection from the world around him. *Where had God been when I needed him? Why would He allow such a thing to happen?* A whisper broke through his burned-out mind.

"Dad? Are you OK?"

No, he wasn't. He was a broken man with a mind hazed from too many pills. Tears streamed down his face, and as he tasted the salt, he realised he was still a man that could feel.

Annabelle could see someone who had shattered into a million pieces and lost every sense of self and pride. His will to follow life's rules had been too much, and his soul had crumpled beneath the weight of the world.

George's words were slow and few, but his face expressed a pain and sorrow that was drowning Annabelle. She had an urge to run, but she knew her father needed her to be strong, as he was no longer able to be. She grasped his hand tight.

"I love you, dad. I don't love what you have done, but I will always love you."

As his eyes met hers, she saw regret. Regret for a life lived with too much pressure. Pressure that grew year by year as he tried to live his father's dream, and not his own. The white-collared job, the white picket fence, and living by the law of the church. Outwardly appearing perfect, yet behind closed doors was a family that inwardly was desperate to share how they truly felt, but ashamed to appear weak by expressing too much emotion. He desperately wanted his family back, but he could sense the hesitation in Annabelle to get too close. Maybe it was too late.

Annabelle noticed her dad's eyes closing as he went back into his dark hole. Trying to find out anything at the moment may prove difficult. How could she broach the subject in a way that provoked no suspicion?

"Dad, may I ask you something? Why did you get so upset with mum?"

His answer was a whisper. "I needed her to love me, and others, so that we may give a child to Eden, to become a part of the perfect world, untainted by the evils of the modern world. She didn't want that, and it made me angry."

"Who is Eden?" Annabelle was curious.

"Not who - it is a place, full of children learning to live in God's pure world. I wanted us to be a part of that, and give to God a child that he may raise away from the evils of our world."

"Does a place like that really exist?"

"Yes, and if your mother would have a baby, we could become a part of that perfect society. But now she is the reason we will all go to hell."

"Tell me about Eden, dad. Where is it?" Annabelle asked softly and slowly so that her dad did not become agitated.

George's eyes filled with tears. "I want to go there so badly. I have always tried to protect you from those that do not believe, but I see I am failing you all. Pastor Neville said those that procreate within the church will create the perfect babies for the new community. We would be a part of something beautiful. It is a tiny town surrounded by tall karri trees. The timber homes stand on wooden stilts overlooking a beautiful lake. The women make clothes, they bake and nurture the children that are the purest forms of God. The men may leave to work and get supplies, but the women and children never step foot outside."

"That sounds perfect. Have you ever been there?"

"No, not yet. I will, though. I have watched videos. Pastor Neville showed me that night I went to the meeting, when your mother was too unwell to come. He had said maybe your mum was not feeling well because she was with child. So he gave me a booklet and showed me the beautiful town of Eden. I was so hopeful, but then your mother told me she just had a virus. Another letdown. It sent me spiralling into sadness and anger." George pulled a crumpled piece of paper out of his pocket and held it up to his heart.

"May I see?"

Annabelle saw a brightness suddenly light up George's eyes. He grabbed her arm hard and started gabbling.

"I want us to go now! God is where our freedom lies. Eden will save the world and our children will be saved!" He was shouting now and his nails dug into her flesh.

A nurse ran over with a guard and tried to calm George's sudden mania, but he was still holding on tight to Annabelle. His eyes were wild and she was frightened. Firmly but gently the nurse spoke to George while the guard eased his grip on her arm. As the nurse sat him down and gave him two small white pills to take, Annabelle quickly picked up the piece of paper she saw George drop in the scuffle.

George continued to rant and scream as he was led away to an isolation room. Annabelle's heart was pounding; she had never witnessed anything so frightening. She found herself crying uncontrollably as another nurse sat with her and explained that her father had developed depression and a mania due to extensive stress. When he got anxious the symptoms increased. He would be calm soon and sleep.

"It's not your fault," the nurse said to Annabelle. "He simply cannot cope with day-to-day life at the moment. Once he stabilises, things will go back to how they were before."

Annabelle's mind was jumbled. *I don't want him back, he is horrible, he is controlling, and he has always been a little weird.* She thanked the nurse and said her goodbyes.

Handel was waiting at the car. He smiled with his usual wide grin. "How's he doing?"

"Not so good." Annabelle described the encounter.

"Whoa, that's not good. Sorry sweetie, no one should have to see their dad that way. Let's get you home."

The tears began again. Handel also had a tear in his eye. This was an emotional time for everyone.

"That piece of paper in your hand of any use to us?" he asked.

"Not sure, I haven't looked at it yet," she replied, tucking it into her pocket. They drove home the rest of the way in silence, both of them thinking about how awful this whole situation had become.

Meanwhile, life went on around them. The rest of the world bustled along with its city rhythm. Car horns honked, sidewalk lights flashed from green to amber to red, people walked hurriedly to where they were going with phones glued to their ears, birds sung their daily songs and the sun moved lower in the sky as the day progressed. Everyone was in their own world, fighting their own demons and singing to their own song.

A PLAN

As they pulled into the driveway, Primrose jumped up from her seat on the veranda and rushed over to Annabelle. As she hugged her, Primrose felt her daughter's body shaking uncontrollably as the tears fell. She realised she should not have placed such a heavy responsibility on her young shoulders. She squeezed her tight, kissed her forehead and looked into Annabelle's eyes. She saw sadness and hurt. How could this man she had loved so much destroy everything they had worked for? Family had been everything to them, and now they were fractured with no way of healing. Oh, how did her life get into such a mess? Her life plan had included structure, not discord and chaos.

Annabelle pulled the crumpled piece of paper from her pocket and passed it to her mother. "Mum, dad had this. He placed it on his heart and started ranting and screaming. It was so frightening. His eyes were vacant at first and then he just looked wired. He became so agitated. Then he dropped this booklet. They gave him sedation and then a guard took him into an isolation room. I could hear him screaming and yelling that he had dropped something that was close to his heart. He was repeating over and over that God is in Eden and our life must continue there, and pounding his fists on the glass door. That man is not the father I knew. He has totally lost his mind. I am not going back there, ever."

"No, I don't expect you to, Annabelle. I am sorry I sent you, it was selfish of me."

Sunnie and Handel joined them.

"We may have a lead," Primrose told them. She showed them the crumpled brochure.

"I think we need to google this address and make a trip to find out if this really is where the 'perfect existence' that your father dreamed of is."

Handel typed in the address. It was an isolated location deep in the southwest, surrounded by dense stands of karri trees. A few timber homes dotted the edge of a large lake. An aerial view showed vegetable plots, animals and sheds. A large timber hall with a cross on the top dominated the landscape, beside a small school and playground.

So this was Eden; the perfect world George was fighting for his family to live. But while we all dream of living a perfect existence, it never has and never will exist. Just as wars have been fought to protect our homeland, smaller wars are fought to claim what we feel is rightfully ours. Instead of guns, our weapons are hatred for others, and the belief that one culture or religion is superior to another. We refuse to see that our differences are what make us unique. We should learn to live harmoniously alongside others, to accept our differences and learn from them. This is what real education is, yet ever since the beginning of time, we as humans have failed miserably in this area.

Eden was simply another war being waged in the modern world - a war against technology, a war against change, and a war that causes division. Just as others had tried before, their little suburban church had been trying to create a perfect 'race' living in a perfect world. For the past ten years, they had been quietly putting their plans into place. But by secretly recruiting and expanding their community through devious behaviours, they were really only exploiting the vulnerable in the cruellest way.

Like any extremists, they needed to be stopped. While Handel knew they needed to call out this ludicrous plan, he also knew they could not do it alone. To expose the cult – and the crimes - they would need to involve the authorities. These were vulnerable people who had been socially isolated; brainwashed into believing they were living with God in their own Garden of Eden, being self-sufficient and living and loving away from the influences of modern society.

But Handel was curious. He wanted to visit this 'idyllic retreat of God' so he could see firsthand how this little cult was existing. They planned to go first thing next morning, leaving in darkness and arriving in darkness, finding a safe place to camp where they could observe the isolated community. Besides, being surrounded by bush enjoying a campfire at night was a beautiful way to bring them all back into the circle of life. They could use the time to remember their roots.

HOME

The sun rose over the eastern horizon behind cotton-wool clouds that softened the morning light and threw splinters of gold onto the faces of the innocent as they sat quietly, heads bowed, reflecting with their Maker. A lithe teenager with milky skin and long dark braids sat playing a guitar that was nestled in her lap. Heavenly sounds rose into the air and mixed with bird-song as she sang to rejoice the beginnings of a crisp clear day.

This is the day that the Lord has made; let us rejoice and be glad in it.

As the chorus began, the cacophony of voices as pure as the morning air drifted into the thick forest. When it was finished, the group quietly scattered to go about their morning chores. Women gathered in the kitchen donning aprons as smaller children laughed and ran into the chicken coop to collect warm fresh eggs. The men gathered together in the main hall to reflect and pray for the wellbeing of their community before conferring about the day's work and agenda for the week ahead.

Meanwhile, the campers hidden in the thick trees stirred, woken by the sound of voices blending with the morning chorus of the kookaburras. The sun filtered patterns like lace over the carpet of the earth as they sipped their tea. The lace of light draped over them, enveloping them in peace as they hid among the tall trees quietly waiting to watch a church creating their own slice of heaven on earth. The silence settled around them as they peered into a world where they had not been invited. Primrose protectively cupped her hands around her swelling belly. She knew what would happen if she did not escape from the church's grasp.

Sunnie draped her arm over her friend's shoulder, and Primrose dropped her head snugly onto it. Where would she be without the help of these free spirits? She realised that those who come into our lives may do so freely, but our meetings seem planned by something greater than ourselves. Perhaps life had its own plan for us, with people coming into our lives at different times to help us grow from both good and bad situations. *What does not kill us makes us stronger* echoed in Primrose's mind, as she breathed in the tranquillity of nature and the protection of the strong karri trees reaching skyward to the sunlight. It is the light that feeds us all, yet some never take the time to benefit from its goodness, trapped in searching for something beyond their reach. These innocent children only know one way; they don't realise they are being hidden from a world that exists beyond the bush. The adults may have the power now, but one day they will start to hear stories about beyond the trees and develop a yearning. Their natural teenage rebellion will lead them to seek to be a part of all that has been kept from them. The rebellious teenager denied is a recipe for disaster. These children are not the first to be manipulated; many religious groups or cults have believed that isolating themselves would protect their offspring from the dangers of the modern world. Yet to clip a bird's wings stops them from flying and takes away their ability to nourish themselves. As parents and role models, we must also allow our growing children to make their own decisions, and hope we have taught them enough to survive to adulthood and to cope in a confusing world full of choices.

Primrose got to her feet just in time to see a tall figure approaching down a lightly trodden path to the small clearing where they had set up camp. He was draped in cloth from his shoulders to his feet, and his hair was long and tied back from his face. Following closely behind was a group of young boys adorned in pure white clothing carrying knives and handmade fishing implements and nets. They must be heading to the estuary not far from here in search of food.

There was something primitive, yet moving, about this image. Males moving in a pack, heading out to hunt and gather for their community. White symbolising purity and the all-male group showing strength in unity and masculinity. The elder leading his young to teach and guide them so they may also lead when they mature. Simple, yet powerful. It exists in the city, yet the image is different – so different that sometimes we forget the power of our example on our children. The world is changing, and to not embrace change creates division and ignorance. Education and the ability to survive in our modern society is paramount.

The campers needed to move quickly. Primrose signalled to the others and they swiftly packed up and jumped into the car, leaving no trace. As they drove away, Handel spoke with authority.

"I'm not sure where we go from here. The way they are living – it's not really wrong. It looks organised, the children appear happy and are learning, they are hurting no one. Yet something feels off. I love country living, being self-sufficient in tune with the land and in harmony with the earth. Some of these old traditions are wholesome and good. But isolating young people from the world and keeping them hidden is wrong and could cause major issues if they have their freedom of choice taken from them.

"They are certainly not the first group to do this, and many have survived and exist in harmony without the so-called evils of modern society. What I don't like is the fact they are hidden and growing their group through the evil manipulation of vulnerable people.

"Primrose, we need to keep you out of sight or they will be after your baby. They believe that because the child is born under their rules, they have full rights to the child. The main thing is to keep you and your unborn child safe. With George in the facility, we have the freedom to move you and your family to safety. Meanwhile, I will somehow infiltrate this group and delve deeper."

Handel took a deep breath. First, it was time to get his own family home. Back to his beloved farm that he inherited from his beautiful Danish father who had taken the huge step to relocate his family to the southwest corner of Western Australia, where they could live by the sea and farm as their family had done for generations. It was a place where both his heart and his soul felt as though they were sitting in a comfortable old armchair; a place where he could really breathe, where he knew he was really home.

****

The drive was quiet as each of them took the time to reflect on what was happening to them. An hour later, the tyres turned onto the gravel driveway and they began to stir. Each member of the Brooks family began to chatter excitedly as they drove towards their home.

A tall, rugged-looking broad-shouldered man in work gear walked down the driveway to meet them. Handel stopped the car and jumped out to hug him, greeting him with a laugh and huge slaps on the back as he hugged him tightly.

"Uncle Louis!" exclaimed Cee, joining the rest of her family as they surrounded Louis with warm embraces. When the excitement died down, Handel introduced Primrose, Annabelle and Christian to his younger brother.

"Louis, we have some city slickers here who need to stay with us for some country air." Handel laughed as he spoke. They all moved towards a beautiful, rambling rammed-earth home surrounded by wildflowers and sheltered by tall gum trees. From its position on the top of a small hill, the ocean could be heard in the near distance. Gulls cried above them and salt air wafted on the breeze. An air of relaxation settled on all of their shoulders. They were home.

The sweet aromas of baking wafted from the large country kitchen, and as they entered, a smiling, apron-wearing woman greeted them with a tray of hot scones fresh from the oven. The huge wooden table was set up with homemade jars of jam and slabs of fresh butter.

"Yum, Auntie Milly, your pumpkin scones. I have missed you so much!" Rae and Cee spoke in unison with warmth and love, and once the tray was on the table, another group hug.

"Welcome home. Time to tuck in and tell me all your news. One thing I do know - we need to celebrate your dad's return to good health!" Laughter, banter and chatter filled the farm kitchen and Aunt Milly and Uncle Louis could not wipe the smiles from their faces as the spirit of the house returned with the laughter.

The children had set out to explore and the elders were sitting in quiet discussion around the kitchen table when a set of tyres were heard heading up the gravel driveway. A large white four-wheel drive pulled to a stop beside the kombi, and a man and a woman both dressed in white stepped out of the car. They looked stern and a little agitated as they strode purposefully towards the front door. Handel signalled for Primrose to go into the bedroom. He walked slowly towards the front door as a knock sounded out.

"Good morning," the man said. "We have reason to believe that you and your family have been camping on our property. We were out for a walk this morning and saw your vehicle parked in a clearing. It is extremely unusual for visitors to find their way to our property, so we followed you to find out why."

Primrose peeked through the keyhole to see two familiar faces. It was Doug and Melissa. George had told her they had left town to sort their problems out and start fresh. That would have been about six months ago. Had Melissa fallen pregnant? Primrose dropped her eyes to Melissa's belly and sure enough, she was. It would seem they had followed the church to Eden and now had a 'divine child' on the way – just as George had wanted so desperately for his own family.

Handel spoke to the couple lightly and with warmth. "Yep, that was us. We took a wrong turn at dusk and found the clearing by mistake. We thought it was a pretty spot to camp and the kids were keen to stop. We didn't see any homes nearby, so thought it would be OK. Sorry - we would not have stopped if we thought it was private property. There was just a small dirt track that led to the clearing, and we settled for the night without tents. We were returning from a long trip up north and the kids had become a bit restless. Sorry again."

"No problems," responded the man. "We have had a few poachers around so we thought we would just check. We have quite a little community, you are welcome anytime you are passing by."

Glancing at each other, the couple made their goodbyes and went back to their car. Handel watched them as they huddled close together, whispering with concerned expressions on their faces.

Primrose returned to the others. "That was Doug and Melissa. They were our friends from church, and we partnered with them in couples therapy. Our 'buddies' in more ways than one, if you get my meaning. They were close to George, and that frightens me. They were here making sure no one discovers their beloved

Eden. I would really like to know who is in control of this community of puritans."

Handel replied. "Well, they have given me an 'in' and I am going to use it. I will give it some time, and then pay the community a visit. I need to find out how safe the group is and what their intentions are for those children. Maybe I can offer my help in any trades they need doing."

"It's a trap," said Sunnie. "No one walks into a secret sect and then walks in and out again. They know we have seen them, and they are ensuring we don't meddle in their ways and cause disruption to their community."

"Maybe you're right," pondered Handel. "I know of a few people who've moved into the forests around here to live reclusive lives. Yet I've never heard or seen this lot out in the local towns, so somehow, they are getting everything they need. Secret sources? This community must be highly organised and wealthy to remain so elusive."

Primrose started to tremble as the reality of the situation hit her. She felt violently ill at the thought of Doug being the father of her child. It was all so twisted and dangerous. Was Melissa's child fathered by George? How could they just uproot their family and leave their old life behind? No one even blinked an eye - they simply moved on. How many other vulnerable families were trapped in Eden? The vulnerable and broken were being targeted to feed Pastor Neville's need for the perfect Christian environment, where he had total control and the outside world could not interfere in any way. It also fed his secret sexual fetish. He was a master manipulator hiding behind the perfect cover - the church.

How could the nuclear Christian family have become so denigrated by society and the church lose control? Pastor Neville had planned his escape by manipulating these near-broken families that were crumbling under society's everyday pressures – including her own. How had she been so blinkered and shut off to the world, despite being educated and intelligent? She had lost the ability to open her mind to other possible ways to live and be happy. If she had not met the Brooks family, she and George would be in that sect right now. How lucky she was! George's mind had broken as Primrose started to question his decisions, and not want to live under his over-controlling patriarchy. He had finally met his match, and it had destroyed his mind and spirit. Now she needed to stand up and expose the darkness that remained.

EDEN

In the place they called Eden, on three hundred acres of heavily forested bushland, a community survived solely off the land and each other's abilities. In addition to the children's home schooling, a school had been set up with two teachers - one who taught the younger children, and one that taught the upper levels. The school was registered, and the teachers held daily structured lessons as a group for an hour.

Each evening, the whole community gathered at dusk to sing around a huge bushfire they called the 'fire of life'. Everyone held a lit candle to signify the light they held within; a light that would help them to lead and live a life full of purity and warmth and, when joined with others, could light the darkest sky. Robed in white, candles in hand, their voices sung out to the heavens resonating off the surrounding hills and filling the forests with the voices of purity and sweet love.

A woman called Penelope led the singing. She truly had the voice of an angel. In her former life, she had been part of a punk band, and had walked the path to destruction. She had been found on the doorstep of the church, unconscious, unkempt, weak and malnourished. Pastor Neville had taken her in, and for that she would always be thankful - if not for the church she would be dead. Penelope had no recollection of those first few months under Pastor Neville's care. But when she finally awoke, she realised she was about to bring new life into this world. Now, living in this idyllic paradise, she sang her praises to God and the new child she would celebrate the arrival of any day. Here she could be the kind of mother she never had, and get the support from all within the community. Eden was a place where you celebrated each new life as one big family. Each new life allowed the love of God to spread among them all. She was filled with abundance and love and shared her gift with all.

The fire burned with ferocity, representing the fire that burned within each and every one of them. They had all escaped a life that was ruled by technology, money and structure, where people had become self-absorbed, narcissistic and driven by self-greed, losing their attachment to the universe. They had even lost all sense of who they were, due to society trying to shift the boundaries and allowing everyone to live solely to please themselves. Nothing was unacceptable. The line of respect was blurring; no one was willing to speak up against the minorities due to fear of being seen as bigoted.

But here at Eden they felt safe, within the boundaries they had created. No one could hurt them. Penelope believed that the true family has a mother who nurtures, a father that is strong and leads and protects, and that parents must lead by example. She believed in living a pure life. She wanted to live with people, to respect them, and to live with nature in a way that is kind to the world. Some may think that to be idealistic, but the community at Eden was living it, and Penelope was happy to have been saved in more ways than one. How they got here may be controversial, but she was happy to live among these chosen ones.

DOUG AND MELISSA

With a new child on the way, Doug and Melissa settled into a quiet life at Eden. Doug had found work on a nearby farm, and Melissa was caring for the children of mothers who worked within the community. The couple had blended in, and no one asked any questions. People came and went in these little coastal towns and everyone was respectful of each other's privacy. When all is said and done, most people settling in small rural towns are trying to escape something, whether it's just city life or more personal issues. No one on the outside knew that most of the people living at Eden had lived through sexual trauma, and that the perpetrator had actually given them their freedom by exiling them to this peaceful place. Despite the rules of their daily existence, Eden provided them with a haven that they had come to feel thankful for. They were free to leave whenever they wished, and Pastor Neville had largely left them to live as they chose.

Yesterday, they had felt the eyes of the outside world upon them. A group of young men who had been out to gather berries and fish for the day had seen a small group camping in a clearing on their land. The men wished to welcome them, but the campers had packed up quickly and left. Clearly, they had not wished to be seen. The community felt they needed to find out why these people were watching them, so Doug and Melissa decided to follow the colourful van. Following from a distance, they arrived at a beautiful property where the hills melted into the sea, the morning sun kissed the ocean, and wildflowers ran free. It seemed the essence of beauty and peace. There seemed no reason to feel threatened, so they drove down towards the ocean breeze.

At the front door, a man clothed in loose, raw cotton pants greeted them with a beautiful fresh smile. He told them his name was Handel, and explained that his family had unintentionally arrived at Eden and were simply looking for a place to camp. Doug and Melissa thought that was a little unusual, as their home was only half an hour from Eden. But he didn't look like trouble. He spoke with an easy manner and offered his services to the community as a tradesman if they ever needed any help. He and his wife Sunnie seemed like fellow earth souls.

Doug and Melissa headed back to Eden, deep in thought. They both believed in loving one another, using as few resources from the earth as possible, and living to sustain life and the planet. The earth is our mostly godly possession, and through respecting it, we honour all we believe in. Tonight the moon would be golden and full, and all Eden will be bathed in its light. The earth would be cleansed once more. Slowly, with each cleansing, the world will become pure and no sin will exist. Tonight, they would all adorn themselves in white and show their unity by bleaching all of their body hair, from top to bottom. The women would be busy within the community as each family unit followed the instructions to dye their hair and bathe in milk in order to bring them closer to purity:

Tomorrow we move one step closer to resembling the angels of the heavens.

We may not have wings but we will endeavour to resemble them in as many ways as possible.

May the light of the world shine through us all.

We are our own light; we create our own perfection.
As the moon shines whole so may we.
Tonight we bathe in white light
Moving towards purity of mind and soul
Uniting our community and leaving no trace of the past.

As the moon replaces the sun and shines a light upon the darkness, we will gather.

Cleanse yourself in milk and adorn yourself in white robes as we gather as one under the light of the moon.

Our white life symbolises a clean slate as a new phase of the month commences.

Cleansing ourselves allows us to live each new day and leave the abuse of the past behind us.

Precisely at 8 o'clock, hundreds of white-clad figures with pale bleached hair moved out of the forest into the clearing and circled the huge bonfire prepared by the men. A group of musicians strummed guitars as hymns of purity sung out into the peaceful bushland and each and every community member danced and celebrated under the spotlight of the moon.

A huge figure with a commanding presence demanded silence and prayer.

"We gather, and we sing life's praises as we endeavour to bathe in the light of the universe. Praise to that which is larger than life itself and all it provides. Sing with joy and freedom as we celebrate purity and light among us all. Let us all live with light in our lives, even under the blanket of darkness. Tonight the moon and stars light our path as a new phase evolves to allow us to leave our abusive past where it belongs. We will forget and forgive the sins of a society that masks evil behind wealth and tradition entrenched by power and greed. We commit to a way of life that is cleansed by nature and its intention for us to enjoy life – not with greed or mass consumerism, but as individuals who learn to live as one with the land.

"May the purity of love and life live within us all. May white light shine bright and cleanse us of all of the sins of life. Lead us under your golden orb to live and grow through each passing phase and realise that life is a cycle. If we learn to move and learn and grow with each phase, life will flourish with purity. Sing with one voice, yet with many harmonies, and together our voices will be strong and resonate among us all. Allow joy to fill you to the brim and overflow so that we may all live with mental strength and clarity.

"Too many of our friends have been destroyed by people who have misled and abused us; and by a modern world that destroyed us both physically and mentally. We as a group are stronger than them and ultimately, they will take the path that will lead to their justice. Let us rejoice in the fire of life and shine bright."

A roar of appreciation erupted as the community began to sing and rejoice to the beauty and harmony of the guitars. *The Sounds of Silence* - a beautiful song - resonated into the night sky as the sound of crickets, owls and the wind drifted into a darkness that was at ease with the glow of the stars and the moon. Then silence, as the white-robed figures silently retreated to their homes to slumber in total peace, knowing they were free of the distractions created by modern man.

Tomorrow the sun would rise again, and the light would also rise within all who partook in the living light celebration.

PEACE

A gentle sea breeze wafted through the open windows of the Brooks' rambling cottage, drifting salt-scented air inside as families slumbered. Sleep here was sound. Both adults and children lived by the clock of the land, infused by nature, allowing them to live without the stress of the sounds of traffic and sirens. There was only the songs of the sea birds and the clucking of the roaming chickens that wandered under the large veranda that sheltered the rustic home. Time moved with the tides, the sun and the moon, and as the days passed, their skin took on a gentle glow as the sun warmed not only their bodies, but their spirits.

The sound of the ocean on the early morning breeze beckoned Rae, Handel and even Annabelle to start the day on the crest of the waves. Primrose and Sunnie quietly rose to put the kettle on and prepare a hearty breakfast of freshly collected eggs.

Primrose was slowly easing into this easy lifestyle, but she knew it could not be sustained for long. She needed income and the children needed stability. Her teaching skills should make it easy for her to find a job. The one complication was the impending closeness of her due date. George had always provided well financially for them, but it had come at a huge cost to their relationship. Now he sat alone and broken, consumed by a dream that would never come true. The family was living comfortably off his sickness insurance for the moment, but she knew that could not last forever.

The kitchen became a hive of activity as the younger children chattered and the surfers returned for a feed. Handel was looking tanned and healthy, his battle with cancer seeming to be fought and won. Life for the Brooks family was returning to what they had created as their 'normal'. Primrose was realising that every-one has their own normal, and we can all learn from experiencing how others lived their lives. *Don't fence yourself in and lock your front door from a world that is bigger than you - it restricts your personal growth and stops your children reaching their full poten-tial.* That was the first big lesson she had learned. She knew she would soon have to find somewhere for her family to find their space to grow. In the meantime, it would soon be obvious that her 'pigeon pair' was to be added to, changing all their lives forever. They had been enjoying spring break, but now Primrose needed to decide whether or not she would stay here and home-school the children. She was not returning to the city, that decision was final, but there were so many big decisions still to be made.

A rap at the front door shook her from her musings. As she opened it, Primrose came face-to-face with two familiar faces. This time she had nowhere to hide.

"Melissa, Doug!" Glad she had thrown on a loose dress, she de-cided it was time to face her challenges head-on. Lies would not get her out of this situation. She smiled and tried to deep-breathe her way through. "What are you doing in this beautiful part of the world?"

"OMG!" yelped Melissa, giving Primrose a warm hug. Primrose hoped she would not feel her swollen belly. That would be her undoing. She could still hide her pregnancy, but Melissa - content and glowing – looked more advanced. She couldn't look Doug in the eye, until she realised that she must let go of that guilt. They had both been manipulated by Pastor Neville.

"We met Handel and he mentioned he had some building and electrical skills," explained Doug, smiling warmly at Primrose. "We are hoping he will come to our community and help us out with some new buildings. Is he around?"

Primrose replied easily. "I think you'll find him putting up new fencing up on the hill. Melissa, would you like to come in while Doug speaks to Handel?" Melissa smiled and nodded, and Doug headed towards the hill separating the house from the beach.

Melissa wondered about Primrose's connection with this place. How had she come to be here? She had heard through the church community that George had had some kind of breakdown, so perhaps it made sense for Primrose to find respite in this peaceful seaside town. But what a coincidence!

Primrose felt she could trust Melissa. She had always been a sweet and kind woman who was devoted to her family. She hoped to find out more about this Eden cult they had escaped to live within.

"We heard George was extremely unwell," ventured Melissa.

"He is not recovering quickly," replied Primrose. "He entered a period of deep depression, which they are trying to get under control. These things can take up to six months before they get the right dosage and combination of medications. It's been a difficult time for us all. Handel and Sunny were our neighbours briefly in the city, and were kind enough to offer their home here as a place for us to rest until George recovers."

"Doug has been very concerned about George," said Melissa. "He knows George was so keen to get his family to a place that believed in traditional family values and would unite you all. He had become determined to take you to a better place. Did he discuss this with you? I think he just wanted you to be in the right 'condition' so that you would be accepted into a new enlightened community. We live there now, and our lives could not be richer or better, in ways we had never imagined. We have a new baby on the way, so for us it was the perfect time to move to where our family would have more freedom.

"I know this must be a shock to you, seeing us so far from the city. We are happy again though. As you can see, I am a fair way along with this pregnancy. How it evolved is not conventional, but we have decided to embrace this baby and raise it in a world away from modern society and its lack of morals."

Primrose's thoughts would not connect with her mouth. Tears built in her eyes as she realised that there are some things in this life we just have to let go. No amount of anguish will change the past, yet how we act in the present moment could change the future.

So forgiveness would be her way forward. *We were all entangled in Pastor Neville's web of deceit, and how I act now could decide whether I escape the deceit or become trapped in it forever.*

Something in Melissa's eyes showed compassion and peace. She did not look like she was living a life tainted by abuse or neglect. Her eyes were clear and she looked content with where she was and how she was living. She reached over the table and placed her hand on top of Primrose's, speaking softly and slowly.

"Doug and I made the decision to move away, as we had been told by the church of a place where families that were expecting could raise a child without the fear of it becoming infected by a world that was spiralling out of control. I was scared, and I knew I also needed to get away from the way we were dealing with our marriage problems. I know you also have been tainted by the church and Pastor Neville's therapy for couples. Believe me though, when I say that where George wanted to take you was a far cry from staying within that church community in the city. He was so torn as to how he could escape with his family when you were not conceiving. Conception was the only way he saw to escape. I know it's not conventional, but for him it was truly the only window open. When you shut that window, you broke his mind.

"We are happy now, and looking forward to bringing this child into a new life and community. We were trapped - not only by the city and its hustle and bustle but by a church led by a bitter twisted human, who in his own perverted way, has led us to a better place."

Unsure of how to respond, Primrose remained silent.

Melissa continued. "We would love to invite you and the children to see our community, but we don't want to allow everyone in as we wish to protect our children. We believe we have learned lessons from the dark side of humanity, and we wish our future generations to be protected from what we have endured.

"Sometimes what we see - the white picket fence, the green lawn, the carefully tended garden beds full of flowers and the welcoming veranda - hide a world inside that is turbulent and disturbed due to the hidden agendas of self-serving, greedy, perverted people who hide under garments that they feel justify their behaviours. Our children will not learn the way we have. Their eyes will be open to the light and mystery of a world that is theirs to learn, free from abuse and hidden doorways."

Primrose took in every word Melissa said, but her eyes were misted by tears and a heavy heart prevented her from speaking. *Did I push my husband to breaking point by not trusting his decisions? Why did he have to be so overbearing and controlling?* She had followed George with trust, but he broke that trust when he forced her to participate in behaviour she was not comfortable with. She could not cope with the sadness, the anger and the control. *Was it really Pastor Neville I should have been angry with, and not George?* When Sunnie and Handel had come into their lives, their laughter, freedom, light and love in times of hardship had shown her another way to live. Even Annabelle and Christian had found a lightness in their spirits that had been weighed down too long by the expectations of their father and an outdated moral code. *Without others, we have no comparison as to how life could be different. It's why generations of families continue to live with their faults and never change.*

Primrose realised she could no longer live the way George wanted her to. Had he realised that too, only to be shunned by those he loved the most? Sometimes we leave things just that little bit too late, and then we lose everything. *Well, I will not live with the guilt of George's downfall. He should have dealt with things in a different way and then perhaps we could all be here together.* Instead, she was sitting here opposite a friend who is about to possibly have George's child and raise it in a cult that she feels is the right way of the world.

It was all just too bizarre and too much for Primrose to handle in her fragile state. She was also about to bring a child into this crazy world, but she needed to make her future one that she and her children would be happy with.

Primrose knew that as parents, we are given both power and responsibility, and we needed to use them to make the best of a complicated world. By living with Sunnie and Handel, she now realised it need only be as complicated as we wish to make it.

She found her voice. "I hear you, and I am glad you have found happiness and peace for your family. I am trying to find that for my changed circumstances. George may be in hospital for a long time, so I need time to adjust. I'm not sure I will ever go back to city life. I love the freedom I have now, so I am thinking I will go back to teaching, and try to live close by to where I am now. I have found a new normal, and I am loving how we are all enjoying it."

The door burst open and everyone arrived at once, bringing laughter and energy into the home. Melissa and Primrose looked at one another, and without words an understanding passed between them. Their past had no bearing on their future, but their families' happiness was something they could make happen.

How they did that was up to them.

ENDINGS AND BEGINNINGS

The wind blew off the ocean, thick with salt. It blew the door open with an air of informality. The wind of change had entered, and it smelled good.

Darkness and light, night and day, sickness and health. All part of life. How you live it is up to you. No one should live with abuse and how you escape it will not erase the hurt, but how you deal with it will change your future.

Today, the future looked like being a happy one. Life could not be better. Primrose, Annabelle and Christian were together, creating a new normal and seeking the changes that would bring them happiness. Annabelle and Christian soon welcomed a baby sister, Eve, and they became regular visitors to the Eden community, where Primrose taught in the tightly knit community.

Sunnie, Handel, Rae and Cee had faced adversity and changed their lifestyle so that Handel could have the best medical attention possible. He had survived and they were able to return to where they were the happiest. The whole family opened their hearts and way of life and found they aligned with the new community at Eden. They came and went and contributed to the community's lifestyle and rituals. Open minds create individuals with a broad perspective.

Sadly, George had taken a path that led him into a deep darkness, and his outlook was not good. He faced a long road with the help of mental health professionals. His poor decisions had led to his family choosing to escape him after years of control and mental abuse. George had lived with too many rules and found life too much. Eventually he took one too many sedatives and left his tragic life. He could not live without his family and had lost the perception of reality. When he lost his family, for him that was the end of life. He no longer had control and that was too much for his mind to bear. Sometimes when that dark place is all-consuming, and the issues too deep, the support from loved ones can't help. For George, the past was just too harrowing and the scars too deep. He was a victim of his upbringing.

Pastor Neville was taken down by the cult he created and was banned from being a part of the place he had created through his perversions. No charges were able to be laid for sexual abuse. But Eden became a haven for those who had survived his abuse. They lived a life segregated from mainstream society and were happy being isolated from a world they did not wish to be a part of.

Life will throw you challenges, it will hurt you, it will make you think, but each of us has only this life to live the way we wish. So open your heart and mind to others. Do what is right for you and your family. Surround yourself with laughter and love, and help others in time of need.

Anyway the wind blows, doesn't really matter. Every storm you pass through will cleanse the earth, and the sun will eventually reappear. And when that light breeze kisses you softly upon your cheek, and you hear laughter on the wind, know that the wind of change will guide you around life's next corner. Where it takes you, is up to you.

ACKNOWLEDGEMENTS

I would like to first and foremost thank my family and friends for believing in me and giving me the encouragement and inspiration to commence this novel.

My admiration and thanks go out to my editor, Ingrid Waltham, who has given her time and expertise in making sure I present to my readers a book I can be proud of. Her suggestions and patience have got me over the finishing line. We have laughed, got off-topic, drank coffee and poured the occasional wine as we pored over this story for the past year.

Thank you for helping me stay committed and allowing my voice to remain authentic and true to my intentions. The journey to publishing has been an amazing test for me personally, in my perseverance and my self-belief.

Thank you to all of you who take the time to read my words.
Vanessa Ward
2021

ABOUT THE AUTHOR

Author | Vanessa Ward
Photo | Justin Ward

Vanessa Ward, nee Matson, grew up enjoying the freedom of the 1960s and 70s in the coastal suburb of City Beach in Western Australia, raised by loving parents who had a zest for music, surf and life in the great outdoors. She now lives not far from her childhood home with her husband John and dog Buddy. Vanessa has three adult children - two sons and a daughter.

This is Vanessa's debut novel, the result of a long-held dream to hold a book she had written herself. It was inspired by her roles as daughter, wife, mother, friend and nanna, and her work as a Registered and paediatric nurse and, currently, as a neurophysiology technologist.

Each of these roles has shaped Vanessa, and their effects on her life are entwined throughout the words in this novel. Her aim was to write a story that would resonate with others, and to challenge their perceptions of the world and the many differences that make us unique.

This book is entirely fiction, but Vanessa's family were her inspiration. Writing it has given her the opportunity to retrospectively muse on her own parenting; she has thought deeply about how she has raised each of her three children through the lens of her beliefs, values, education and life experiences. She realises that she could only have done it that way; and it was a result of her own fortunate upbringing. Observing how differently other families behaved, Vanessa realised that no one way is perfect - yet sometimes, being imperfect is OK too.

www.ingramcontent.com/pod-product-compliance
Lightning Source LLC
Chambersburg PA
CBHW030626120726
47904CB00006B/2056